The First Tackle
Girls with Game

Published by Wombat Books, 2022
P. O. Box 302
Chinchilla Qld 4413
Australia
www.wombatrhiza.com.au
admin@wombatrhiza.com.au

© Rikki-Lee Arnold, 2022

Cover by Carmen Dougherty
Layout by Wombat Books
ISBN: 978-1-76111-081-8

A catalogue record for this book is available from the National Library of Australia

RIKKI-LEE ARNOLD

Wombat Books
Stories you'll want to share

CONTENTS

This book is dedicated to Mum, Danica, Chloe, Grandma, Noo-Noo, Emily Hayes, and ALL the powerful women in my life.

CHAPTER ONE

MY RANDOM PREDICTION

With a football tucked firmly under my arm, I step past Jimmy's basketball in the middle of the backyard, dodge Tommy's bike and race towards the trees that line the fence.

'And Kalyn Ponga, he's put Dani Murphy through a gap … she steps one, steps two … AND SHE'S OUT IN THE OPEN! NO ONE CAN CATCH HER NOW!'

I put the ball down, scoring my try, raise my arms above my head and start doing my victory dance.

'It must be hard work commentating your own moves like that,' a voice breaks through my celebration. 'Better not let Grandma catch you with that ball in your hands.'

'Wha—'

I whip around, my cheeks going red as I realise I'm not alone. Jimmy is leaning up against the doorway to the backyard, arms folded across his chest and a massive smile on his face.

'Those moves weren't bad, kiddo,' my big brother says. 'Not bad at all.'

'Oh … thanks,' I say. 'I … I didn't know you were there.'

'I've been ordered to escort you to dinner. Grandma asked me to come find you.' Jimmy raises his eyebrows and tilts his head, staring pointedly at the football on the ground.

Without thinking I raise my hand to the scar under my chin, a bubble of guilt starts in my tummy.

'Well, lucky she sent you instead of coming out here herself,' I say, forcing a small smile onto my face.

'Ah kiddo,' he says as he walks out into the yard, scoops up the footy and passes it to me, 'don't stress. I'm not going to tell on you.'

'Mmm,' is all I can manage. Easy for him to say. I know it's risky to play football when Grandma is home, but I just had that itch today. I saw the footy sitting in the yard and I couldn't ignore it.

'So, how does it feel playing with the one and only, Kalyn Ponga?' he says, changing the subject with a cheeky grin and a wink. 'Don't feel like you're betraying your beloved Brisbane Broncos by joining the Newcastle Knights?'

'No way!' I laugh. 'We were playing for the Maroons, of course.'

Kalyn Ponga is my favourite player in the NRL but the Broncos are my favourite team. I hug the ball close to my chest as we walk across the grass. The sky is a pretty mix of blue and pink today, like a sherbet lollipop. I love this time of year. It's the first day of autumn—the very best season. It starts to get nice and cold, but not too cold. I'm so glad I don't have to do swimming at school anymore and I can start wearing my jeans again. And, of course, it means the NRL is starting very soon. The greatest sport of all.

'Is ... is it okay for me to have a favourite player outside of the Broncos?'

'Of course it is, you big dork,' Jimmy says. I gently shove him and he pretends to fall to the ground, clutching at his arm as if I've hurt him. I start laughing, until—

'You only like Kalyn Ponga because you think he's good looking,' an annoying voice pipes up from the doorway. This time it's my younger brothers, the troublesome twins, Sammy and Tommy. I much prefer when they're busy with Minecraft. It usually means they leave me alone.

Tommy starts batting his eyelids at me and Sammy makes kissing noises.

'I do not!' I say, my face getting hot. Stupid boys.

'Oi, go wash your hands you two,' Jimmy says. Tommy pokes his tongue out and they both race away.

'They wouldn't say that to you,' I tell Jimmy as I watch Tommy and Sammy disappear down the hallway. 'They only say it to me because I'm a girl.'

'Kiddo,' Jimmy says, crouching in front of me to look into my eyes. 'Don't listen to them. They're seven. What on earth do they know? Nothing. Trust me. Now, as your older, wiser, funnier and much better-looking brother, I know for a fact that you like Kalyn Ponga for his football skills and nothing else. I know it, you know it and that's all that matters. Right?'

'Right,' I say with a tiny smile.

'Ok, good. Now … last one to the dinner table is a dirty, rotten Manly player!'

Jimmy leaps up, catching me off guard and runs to the door. I race after him laughing, knowing I can't keep up. But that's ok. I might have ended up with two annoying brats for little brothers, but I got pretty lucky in the big brother department.

After I wash my hands, I sit down for dinner with my family, plonking myself next to Jimmy, with Sammy and

Tommy across from us. Grandma usually sits on the other side of me at the head of the table while Dad is down the other end. It's just the six of us and it has been for a long time.

Grandma walks in with the last bowl for dinner—a huge serving of mashed potatoes—and puts it down between a dish of green beans and a platter of lamb chops.

'Dig in, everyone,' she says, taking her own seat.

'It looks delicious, Grandma,' I say. 'Thank you!'

'Hey Grandma,' Sammy butts in, 'is Dani allowed to play rugby league if she plays it by herself?'

I look up from the chop that I was ready to tear into. It may sound like an innocent question, but from Samuel Jordan Murphy, it is not. I glare at him as he smiles at me, shovelling potato into his mouth. I don't know anyone who loves food more than Sam.

'I'm not sure I understand what you're saying, Sam,' Grandma says. 'How can she play by herself?'

'Oh, we just saw her in the backyard with a footy, Grandma. She was pretending to score a try.' Now it's Tommy's turn to chime in as he pushes his food around his plate. These two are dead meat.

Grandma looks at me over the top of her purple glasses. Dad meanwhile just looks up at the ceiling while turning a chop over in his hands.

'Is that true, Daniella?' Grandma asks.

'Well, I—'

'It's ok, Grandma,' Jimmy interrupts. 'It's just running when she's playing by herself like that. She's not tackling or anything. Obviously.'

'Hmmm … well, okay then. I guess that's okay. But Daniella, I've told you before that girls don't play rugby league. It's too rough and too dangerous. You can watch it, but you cannot play. You're a lady, not some kind of thug.'

She reaches over and brushes my hair back off my face.

'It's not for my little girl,' she says, cupping my cheek.

'Yes, Grandma,' I mumble as I fiddle with a green bean. But really I want to shout from the rooftops that ALL I want to do is play rugby league. Just like Jimmy and Tommy and Sammy. It's what I dream of every night in those moments right before I go to sleep. I've just never really had the guts to tell anyone.

I may love rugby league as much as my brothers (maybe even more) but I am the only one who is not allowed to play it. Grandma has no issues with me watching it. She says I'm safe in the stands or on the couch. But playing it? As a girl? No way. 'Absolutely not, Daniella.' Not in the backyard with Jimmy, not at the Banford Saints rugby league club where my brothers play. I tried to give it a go once when I was eight at the Banford Saints' end-of-season party but I cut my chin open on some kid's boot and needed stitches. That was when Grandma officially banned me. The boys get little injuries all the time, but Grandma said she couldn't bear to see 'her little girl' hurt. Now I'm ten, nearly eleven, and all I'm allowed to do is watch.

I sigh and touch the little scar under my chin again as the conversation moves on. I love Grandma a lot, but she's really tough, especially on me. She moved in with us five years ago when my mum passed away. Mum got really sick when I was little, not long after Sammy and Tommy were born. I can't remember too much about Mum except that she had thick, dark hair, just like mine. Dad says I am the spitting image of her, right from my long legs to the freckles on my nose (but he says I have his hazel eyes and quiet nature). I think I remind both Dad and Grandma of her.

Grandma said she had to live with us to help Dad and to make sure I wasn't the only girl in the family or I'd become too much like my brothers. She said Mum had been her little girl and now I was too. But, as much as Grandma tries, I'm exactly like my brothers.

'All right team, tonight's the night,' Dad says from his

end of the table. He wipes his mouth and hands and gets up to collect a pile of papers and pens from the kitchen bench. I get a buzz through my body, like an electric shock. It really is rugby league time again!

'It's season prediction time,' he says, passing the sheets out to everyone, even Grandma. 'I want to know who you think will win the NRL premiership this year, who will get the wooden spoon, who will be Dally M Player of the Year, who will win State of Origin and your most random prediction. Same drill as always—your answers are sealed and not opened again until the day after the grand final. The person with the most correct answers wins $20.'

It's a little family tradition we do. I have never won but this year could be my year.

'I don't know why you make me do this, Leo,' Grandma says, smiling at Dad. 'I only care about the Cowboys, no one else.'

'I reckon the Roosters have it in the bag this year, Dad,' Jimmy says as Dad playfully swats him over the head with his own piece of paper.

'Enough of that now,' he smiles.

'Already jinxing the Chooks. Tut, tut, Jimmy,' I laugh.

The phrase 'in the bag' is banned from our house because Jimmy said it during a Roosters game a few years ago when they were winning by four points. They ended up losing it by two points and ever since it's been seen as a curse. Dad is a Roosters fan, Jimmy goes for the Broncos just like me, Grandma cheers for the Cowboys (but doesn't really watch much NRL outside of that), and Sammy and Tommy like the Bulldogs.

I look down at my sheet and think about my answers carefully.

Premiers? Broncos. Always. I'm too biased.

State of Origin winners? Queensland. Of course.

Dally M Player of the Year? Kalyn Ponga. For sure.

Wooden Spoon? Hmmm ... maybe the Dragons.

Random prediction? I look around the room as everyone is busy writing.

'How do you spell 'Warriors'?' Tommy asks.

I look back at my own piece of paper.

My random prediction is that I will play rugby league this year, I write.

It's just a wish, but I guess you never know what could happen. I fold the piece of paper up tightly, write my name on it, close it with sticky tape and hand it to Dad with a smile. He puts all the predictions in an envelope, seals it and puts it in a cupboard above the fridge where they will stay until after the grand final. I have a good feeling about this one.

Yeah. This year could really be my year.

CHAPTER TWO

THE GIRL WITH RED HAIR

Something has changed in my world. Something massive. Just five days ago, Grandma was telling me that girls don't play rugby league. Today, however, I know differently.

I'm hiding behind a ginormous gum tree that stands near the goalposts while Jimmy trains at the Banford Saints rugby league ground. I tip my head way back just to see the top of the tree, with the green leaves dancing in the breeze. It's the perfect hiding spot. No one can see me. No one will find me. It's just the way I need it.

I carefully peer out from behind the thick, pale trunk and take a sneak peek at my surroundings. An old deflated football lies forgotten at my feet. Beyond that, a bunch of kids run in circles screaming as they play tiggy.

'You're it!' one grubby kid screeches at another.

As fun as it looks, I don't have time to play games like tiggy. Not today. I have some important business to deal with.

Some parents stand in a huddle near the canteen, a checklist in the hands of one of the mums. A rather big man with a white moustache barks orders at his players on the field. The players all get down on their hands and knees and start doing push ups. One boy counts as they go. There is noise all around me, yet I am as quiet as a mouse. My heart thuds. It's time to move.

I slip out from behind the gum tree and run as fast as I can. A twig snaps under my foot as I dodge some training cones left on the grass. I finally make it to the smelly dressing sheds and slip inside, pressing my body against the wall. The stink of sweat and Dencorub fills my nostrils. Hopefully no one spotted me. Breathe in. Breathe out. I feel like a super-secret spy or something. I need a new identity, like Agent Murphy. Uncovering all the big secrets that the Banford Saints have. I take another deep breath and look out the door.

It's almost like any other Tuesday afternoon. Jimmy is running back and forth across the green field with his teammates from the Banford Saints' under-16s team. He's the hooker and the captain. Normally I sit in the ute with Dad and do my homework and we talk about our day while Jimmy trains.

But today I had to make a quick escape. I told Dad I needed to go to the toilet but I'd actually seen something I'd never seen before—or should I say, *someone* that I had never seen before.

I just had to get a closer look and I didn't want Dad to stop me.

She is tall—even taller than me and I'm the tallest kid in the fifth grade. She has thick, strong legs. Mine are long and sticklike. Her skin is darker than mine and her eyes are brown while mine are hazel. She has curly red hair, as bright as fire. Mine is black and not curly, just bushy—'always a mess' Grandma says.

But she is a girl and she is playing rugby league. I have never seen her before—or any girl playing rugby league for that matter. Watching her makes me feel funny. I have butterflies in my tummy and my heart is pounding even harder against my chest. I can barely breathe.

She's my sign. My proof. It can't be a coincidence.

The girl with the red hair reminds me of Wonder Woman. I'm going to have to write to my school pen pal, Amina, and tell her all about it. She will love that I've found a real-life superhero!

I'm still hypnotised by her when I spot someone coming my way. Oh no. I have to hide again. Of all the people, he cannot see me right now. I step back into the sheds, tiptoe towards the back of the room and look around for a hiding place.

'Are you trying to be creepy or is that just who you are, Dani?' a voice snarls.

Too late.

I turn slowly, ready to face my nemesis. Not only have I failed on my first mission as a super-secret spy, but I've run into the biggest bully at Banford State School, Mitch Delaney.

'Hi Mitch,' I say, looking down at my scuffed black school shoes. All my excitement disappears.

'What do you think you're doing? This is a change room for boys,' he snaps, hands on his hips.

'Well, there's a girl out there,' I mumble, walking back to the doorway to point towards the training fields. 'I was just watching her.'

'What?' he laughs, running to the small dressing sheds window to have a look, his eyes wide with surprise. 'Do you think she's lost?'

Every year my school report card comes home to Dad and Grandma and it says that, 'Daniella is a good student. She does all her work well. She is however a little quiet and does not participate in many class discussions'.

Dad calls that 'shy'. But, no matter how shy I am, when something makes me mad, I can't hold my feelings in. Dad calls that 'quick to anger'. I glare at Mitch and I can feel my temper rising.

'You're just scared she might be better than you,' I whisper sharply back at him.

He laughs. Mitch Delaney hates it if someone is better than him at something. I know he doesn't like me because I'm taller than him and can run faster.

'Nah, girls can't tackle,' he says back to me, sticking his chin out.

I clench my fists. In my head, I picture myself like one of those cartoon characters with my face all red and steam coming out of my ears. Mitch Delaney is easily the meanest boy in our grade.

Even though he is shorter than me, he is bulky. He has spiky blonde hair, brown eyes and a pointy face like a rat. Usually I can avoid him at school as he prefers to pick on some of the other kids and I do everything I can to stay out of his way.

I wish I could tell him what I really think of him, but the words aren't coming out. Then I hear the familiar crunching noise of footy boots hitting the concrete ground outside the sheds.

'What's going on?' Jimmy asks, panting from his tough training session.

I instantly relax … Jimmy's always there when I need him. Mitch just smirks at me.

'Just talking about school,' he says. 'I'll catch you tomorrow, Dani.'

Mitch grabs his boots and pushes past me to leave the sheds. I still feel angry but as soon as I see Jimmy with some grass sticking out of his dark hair and mud smeared on his cheek, I can't help but smile. He walks forward, puts his hands on my shoulders and pushes them back.

'Walk tall, stand proud, Murphy,' he says with a smile of his own. He says that to me a lot. He thinks I hunch my shoulders too much because of how tall I am. But he also says I shouldn't hide it, that I should be proud of my height. That's why he's my favourite person.

'C'mon kiddo,' Jimmy says as he puts his arm around my shoulders. 'It's time to go home.'

He steers me out of the sheds and my hair tickles my cheeks as the cool wind blows across the fields. I can smell the hot chips cooking in the club canteen and can see little puffs of dirt rise around my shoes with every step I take. As we walk to the car, I stare around the Banford rugby league grounds trying to find the red-haired girl again, but I can't see her. She was training with the under-

12s team—that is one year older than I am. They always train at the same time as Jimmy's under-16s.

'Hey Jimmy, did you see the girl who was training with the under-12s?' I ask.

'She was pretty good, huh?' he says, nodding.

I smile. I knew he would be as impressed as I was.

'She really was. Grandma always says girls shouldn't play rugby league, but she must be wrong. If that girl can play, surely we can all play. Surely I can play! I can't wait to tell her!'

Jimmy smiles back and ruffles my dark, messy hair.

'Good luck kiddo,' he says. 'You know Grandma, it's her way or the highway.'

I think about how angry and scared she looked that time I needed stitches—the day she decided I couldn't play rugby league at all. She put her foot down, Dad did nothing, and the rest is history. I touch my chin. But this time, maybe for the first time ever, Grandma is wrong.

'Well, maybe one day she'll let me play,' I say. 'Maybe I just have to convince her. Maybe one day I can be just like you … and that girl, of course!'

Jimmy smiles and puts his arm back around my shoulders as we reach the car.

'Dani, if anyone can do it, I know it's you.'

As I buckle up my seatbelt, I realise I didn't solve my

mystery. It's definitely a failed mission. I still don't know who that girl is but I feel tingles in my chest, like I've uncovered a big clue in an even bigger case. I guess I'm going to have to be a super-secret spy for a bit longer.

CHAPTER THREE

TAKING A CHANCE

'Out here, out here!'

The call echoes down the street as I walk home from school. It's been just one day since I saw the girl with the red hair and I was barely able to concentrate on anything Mrs Crawley said in class today because all I could think of was the plan that kept me up all night long.

Even during maths—my favourite subject besides P.E.—I was daydreaming about becoming a rugby league player, just like the girl with red hair. I kept an eye out for her at school in case she was a new student, but I didn't see her at all.

I told Dad and Grandma all about her last night after we got home from training.

'You should have seen her,' I said. 'She was so strong and some of the boys were struggling to keep up with her. Maybe that means girls can play, Grandma?'

'Mmm … that's enough of that for now, Daniella,' Grandma replied. 'So Jimmy, how was your English exam today?'

Dad said nothing and just gave me a little smile as he bit into his corn cob, but that was it. He always leaves the talking to Grandma.

Grandma may have brushed me off, but the mystery girl has still been on my mind all day and as I get closer to Windemere Park—the best park in Banford—I feel like I could explode with excitement. The sun's out, the sky is blue, and the birds are chirping. I couldn't have asked for better conditions for what waits around the corner.

Nearly every afternoon after school, Tyrone Walker and all his friends come down here to play a game of league. Nearly every afternoon I just walk past, head down, right in the direction of my brown brick house. But today, all I can see is the red-haired girl's face. All I can think is, what would she do? Would she just walk past and ignore them?

I don't think she would. I came up with the plan last night as I lay awake in bed. If she can do it, I can do it too. So, today I will. It's time to act on my goal. I even wore

19

my Banford sports uniform, ready for action. Grandma never needs to know.

'Fifth tackle,' Bobby Jones calls the end of a set as I walk by the swings.

And then before I can stop myself—

'Hey Tyrone,' I yell out.

I freeze. I'm actually doing this. I'm actually following my plan. It's like I couldn't hold the words in. They just escaped from my mouth. They burst right out of me! Now I feel like I could puke. Tyrone turns around.

'Dani?' he asks, like he hasn't seen me in years, even though we're on lunchtime clean up together this week.

My legs are shaking so much and I feel like running away but again the mystery girl with the red hair pops into my brain. Tyrone walks over to me. I have to be brave.

'Hey … do … do you think … do you think ...' I say. I grip the straps of my school backpack. A trickle of sweat slips down the back of my neck. I gulp.

Tyrone frowns.

'Um, are you ok?'

'Do you think I could play with you today?'

It explodes out of me again. Tyrone's eyebrows shoot upwards and his mouth makes a little 'o'. Then I hear a loud laugh come from behind him.

'What did you just say Dani?'

It's Mitch Delaney. Of course. I feel hot all of a sudden and it's like my cheeks are burning.

'I …' I look back at Tyrone who is staring at me as if I just asked him a difficult maths question (it might be my favourite subject, but it's definitely not his).

'You can't play with us,' Mitch says and some of the other boys join in his laughter.

'Never mind,' I mutter. I pull tight on my backpack and go to turn away as tears prick my eyes but Tyrone puts a hand on my shoulder.

'Oi,' he says to his friends, 'leave her alone. Let her play.' He looks back at me. 'Have you played before?'

'No.'

'Ah, ok. Well, of course you can play. But be careful. No crying if you get hurt.'

I nod. I must show him (and everyone else at the park, especially Mitch) that I can do it. I quickly blink away my tears to show him I'm serious. No crying. I have always liked Tyrone. He is one of the nicest boys in my class and I think he has a crush on my best friend, Bethany, so he sometimes hangs around us at morning tea. Now he's taking a big chance on me. I dump my backpack with the rest of the school bags and run over to him.

'You can be on my team,' he says. 'Can you handle the wing? It's the position where you stand on the edge of the field and you mostly finish off plays and—'

'Gosh, give me some credit, Tyrone!' I exclaim. 'I know what a winger is.'

He laughs.

'Okay, sorry, my bad.'

I smile and run across the freshly mown grass to take my place. It's no fullback position (the number one jersey, just like Kalyn Ponga), but I guess I have to start somewhere and Tyrone knows I am the fastest girl in our grade. You need to be fast to be a winger.

The butterflies come back and they are going wild. Mitch Delaney is captain of the other team and he walks over to his best friend Bobby Jones and whispers something in his ear. They smirk. I frown back.

'Kick off already,' yells Max Thompson.

Bobby places the ball on the tee, takes a few steps back, sticks his arm in the air, darts forward and boots the ball.

Right. Towards. Me.

Wingers and fullbacks usually catch the kicks, but I know this one was especially targeted at me. I stand under the ball as it swirls high in the air. I steady my feet and stick out my arms in the same way I have seen Kalyn Ponga and all the other footballers do it on the TV. It comes tumbling down … I think I've got it … no wait,

I'm sure of it!

The football hits my forearms hard and bounces straight off me, onto the ground. My cheeks have already turned red again before Mitch and all his teammates start howling with laughter. My arms are stinging. My heart sinks. That was a hard kick. I sigh and can hear some of my own teammates groan. But Tyrone is at my side faster than a bullet.

'It's fine,' he says. 'Get your head up and move on.'

'Alright guys,' he calls to the team, 'one set to defend!'

He sticks up one finger in the air, like the pros do on TV. I give myself a shake off. I turn around and find myself marked up against Bobby Jones. While Mitch might be bulky and strong, Bobby is more like me. He's thin and gangly, but not quite as tall.

'Nice catch, freak face,' he says. I frown again.

The play starts and Mitch's teammate Harry swings the ball out our way. Two tackles later and Mitch turns to pass to Bobby. I sprint forward, thinking about the way Cowboys player Jason Taumalolo can put on a bone-crunching tackle. I think about the red-haired girl and how she did everything the boys did at training yesterday.

Then I drive my shoulder into Bobby's stomach, wrap my arms around him and push him into the ground. It's like an explosion has gone off. My team bursts into cheers from behind me and Tyrone pulls me off Bobby, who has gone white with shock.

Mitch looks like someone has slapped him across the face but Tyrone looks like his birthday and Christmas has come all at once. The way I feel is better than anything I could dream of in those moments before I go to sleep.

'If I knew you could tackle like that, I would have asked you to play ages ago!' he says.

I'm about to cry again, but this time because I am so happy. I hold back my tears though and give him a big grin instead. Bobby gets up to play the ball and this time Mitch passes the ball away from me. Mitch glares over at me one more time before running off. But I don't care.

Nothing can ruin this day for me. Not the dropped ball, not Mitch Delaney. I'm playing rugby league.

CHAPTER FOUR

SKINNED KNEES AND
WHITE LIES

I'm very late. I know it. I was so tired by the time the game ended that I wasn't in the mood to restart my walk home. That was until I checked my watch and saw I was supposed to be home half an hour ago.

The image of Grandma's cranky face has given me a huge burst of energy! Now I'm running down the street, my school bag slapping into my back. Windemere Park is about a five-minute walk from my school and is the next street over from my house. As I run, I see all the families getting home from long days at school and work—there are so many families that live in Banford, a small town near Brisbane in Queensland. Dad calls our street a 'suburban paradise', whatever that means. I think it's because there's a lot of trees and green lawns. Dad is a builder, but he also loves gardening and looking at other people's gardens.

I turn the corner and see my long, winding brick driveway. A plain brick driveway and a plain brick house. It sounds boring, but I actually love our home. It's only one storey (Bethany's house has three storeys!) but it's a really wide house and we have a massive backyard to play in. Out the front is Dad's favourite part—his hedges. I don't get it, but he loves them.

I finally reach our front door but stop before I open it. I take a deep breath in. It's not that I'm afraid of Grandma. I'm really not. She's not *that* scary. But she can be tough on me and I hate disappointing her. She is the one in charge of all discipline. Maybe, just maybe, she hasn't noticed I'm late.

Dream on, Dani. Here goes nothing.

I open the front door as quietly as I can and then close it softly behind me. I push my white school joggers off and tiptoe down the hallway in my green socks. I can smell Grandma's famous, mouth-watering spaghetti sauce coming from the kitchen and hear the sound of the television, which means she's 'watching her stories' while cooking our dinner.

That's what she calls her shows anyway. Dad just calls

it 'trashy TV'. I have almost made it to my bedroom door when the wooden floorboards creak underneath my foot. Uh oh. They have given me away.

'Daniella Murphy,' Grandma's voice booms from behind me.

I slump my shoulders and turn around. Her arms are crossed over her splotchy purple apron and there is a frown on her face.

'You are late,' she says as her blue eyes take in my messy appearance.

She looks me up and down and then her eyes go wide. She looks almost scared for a second. I don't look down but I know she has seen my bloody knees. I skinned them in a tackle. It didn't hurt at all, but I know they don't look very good.

'Daniella Grace Murphy!' Grandma says sternly.

'Y-yes, Grandma?' I ask, pretending nothing is wrong and giving her my full attention.

'Firstly, why are you so late? I was getting worried. And secondly, just what on earth have you been doing with yourself? Your hair is a mess, you have dirt on your school shirt and blood on your knees!'

'I … I tripped over?'

'Are you asking me or telling me?'

I gulp. If she knew what I had actually been doing

then she'd get really mad.

'I'm sorry, Grandma,' I say. 'I didn't mean to be late. I just decided to go on the swings at the park with Bethany and I swung too high and fell off. That's all. I really am sorry.'

Grandma frowns even deeper.

'I thought Bethany didn't walk home with you on Wednesdays because she has dance lessons?'

'They were cancelled today,' I blurt out the lie. I don't like it, but the words are out there before I can stop them. 'Her teacher is sick.'

'Hmmm … okay. Well, go get changed out of your uniform. Bring it to me so I can wash that dirt off immediately and then I will clean up your knees. And no more stopping to play in the park after school. You need to be home on time or I worry.'

'Yes Grandma,' I say.

She walks away and I feel yucky in my tummy. I know lying is wrong. I never lie, especially to Grandma. But the truth definitely would have made her very angry. Feeling guilty, I go into my room and do exactly as she says. I change into one of Jimmy's old hand-me-down Broncos jerseys and a pair of denim shorts.

I take my green and yellow school clothes out to her and leap up onto the kitchen bench so she can clean my knees. While the kitchen smells like her tomatoey spaghetti sauce, she smells like lavender. It's a nice smell and one that always makes me feel calm. Her light brown hair is brushed neatly into a bun on the top of her head and her purple glasses have slid down her nose slightly. Purple is her favourite colour.

She gently tends to my knee, rubbing it with red antibacterial cream. It actually makes it look like I have been bleeding heaps more than I really did. It's pretty cool. They're my battle scars. That's what Dad calls any injuries we get. She then sticks a couple of band aids across my knees.

'I hate to see you hurt,' she sighs. Then she leans in to give me a kiss on the forehead. 'There you go my girl.'

She gives me a funny look as I jump off the bench. Maybe she knows I have been lying or maybe I am imagining it because I feel bad for lying. But I swear from this moment on, I won't lie to her again. I will just have to be more careful when I play my super-secret rugby league.

I walk into the computer room and sit down at the desk. I have some homework to do but I also want to see whether I have any new emails from Amina.

Amina lives in New South Wales but our schools set us up as email buddies as part of a project last year. Everyone in her grade was matched with someone in my grade. I was so lucky to get Amina. She is really cool and interesting, so we always have something to talk about. She loves maths (just like me!), superheroes (like Wonder Woman!), comic books, drawing and board games. She was born in Sydney but her parents are actually from a faraway place called Iraq.

Amina is Muslim and wears a hijab on her head, which is like a veil. The first time she wrote to me, she sent me a picture of her wearing a bright pink one. She has long, dark hair, big green eyes, really rosy cheeks and she is quite short. She is an only child so she always wants to hear stories about my big, loud family.

Amina also plays soccer for her local club and doesn't really know anything about rugby league. But her soccer is what I always want to hear stories about. Apparently heaps of girls play soccer with her and she doesn't even have any boys in her team.

She has lots of friends and now I am one too. The project ended last year but we still email each other all the time. Like today. As I log on to the computer, I see one new message from Amina.

To: dani.number1@mailbox.com
From: soccer.star@mailbox.com
Subject: BIG NEWS!
Hey Dani! Guess what?!?!?! I have just

found out we have some new girls in our soccer team this year. New friends! Yay! I'm super excited because we really need some more people after Britney moved away last year. Fingers crossed they are really nice (and also good players of course!!!). All I'm doing is counting down to the new season. I hate when soccer isn't on. But I'm practicing heaps too. What's new with you?!?! How did your big maths test go last week? I bet you did really well. You're the smartest maths nerd I know (besides me hahaha). How are you and how are all your brothers? Did you see a new Batman movie is coming out soon? I can't wait!! You're the only friend I have who loves superheroes as much as me. Hope to hear from you soon! Amina.

I look over my shoulder, back towards the kitchen. I can still hear Grandma's stories playing on the TV and the clinking of spoons and pots and pans as she moves around. I turn back to the computer and start typing up a storm. I have to tell Amina what happened today. I also still have to tell her about my 'Wonder Woman'—the girl with the red hair!

To: soccer.star@mailbox.com

From: dani.number1@mailbox.com

Subject: BIGGER NEWS!!

Hey Amina! I have the BIGGEST secret to tell you!!! But it has to stay a secret. You can't tell anyone … even though we don't know any of the same people hahaha. But … are you ready???(DRUM ROLLLLLL) I PLAYED RUGBY LEAGUE TODAY! I know you're probably staring at the screen with your mouth wide open right now but it's true! I'm not playing with a club like my brothers do or like you do with soccer, but I played in the park today with some boys from school and it went really well. I even made a HUGE tackle! I've always wished I could and I finally did it because I saw a girl training with the under-12s team yesterday. She was just like WONDER WOMAN! Except with red hair. Can you believe it?! If she can do it, why can't I? I've never had such a big secret before. My Dad and Grandma don't know about it yet. But I had to tell someone. I will probably tell Bethany too. And maybe Jimmy. I guess I'm not very good at keeping secrets hahaha. Anyway, I have to go! But I hope to hear from you soon. Dani. PS – The maths test was easy peasy!! What are you learning about in maths at the moment? PPS – I AM SO EXCITED FOR NEW BATMAN!

I wish we could watch it together. You should totally visit Queensland! PPPS - I hope your new soccer teammates are nice too. But I bet they can't play better than you!

I quickly hit the send button before Grandma could spring up behind me and see what I have written. It feels so good to tell someone my news. After dinner I will also ring Bethany (because she actually is at her dancing class right now, despite what I told Grandma) and tell her too. I just can't keep it in.

I hear the front door open and close.

'I'm ho-ome,' Jimmy calls through the house.

He walks past the computer room in his dark blue school uniform (he's in grade 11 at the nearby high school, St Aidan's College), ruffles my hair and goes into his bedroom. I know I will eventually tell Jimmy too but I have to make sure no one overhears, not even Sammy or Tommy because I know for sure one of those brats will dob on me.

Then, I am struck by an idea. It's so simple, I can't believe I didn't think of it earlier. Spies have all kinds of gadgets when they're on a job, including computers! They have to research for their cases all the time and maybe I can do that too.

Maybe I can solve my little mystery and find the name of the red-haired girl who was training with the Banford Saints yesterday. I would love to be able to meet her and tell her that I want to play rugby league too.

It's Agent Murphy time.

I bring up a search bar on the computer and type in 'girl playing rugby league'. All of a sudden the screen is filled with pictures. But they are not pictures of my mystery girl. It is so much more. There are all kinds of girls playing rugby league—high school kids, women, girls my age, even teeny kids who are much younger than me. I scroll down the page. There is picture after picture after picture.

I realise I am not breathing. There are even women in Australian jerseys, just like the men wear when they play for the Kangaroos. I feel a bit silly. How did I not know about this?

'*Girls don't play rugby league. It's too rough and too dangerous,*' Grandma's voice echoes in my head.

'*Do you think she's lost? Girls can't tackle,*' Mitch Delaney's voice comes through next.

'*You can't play with us!*'

I didn't know because I have always been told it was impossible. No one let me know. I didn't know because I just believed all those voices. I never saw what I could be.

Until now. I thought the red-haired girl must have been the only one but I'm so wrong.

I feel like I'm stuck to the chair and buzzing with energy all at the same time. I still can't see the red-haired girl in any of these pictures but now I know that heaps of girls play rugby league!

'Daniella, what are you doing?' Grandma suddenly asks from behind me.

I quickly close the page.

'Nothing,' I say.

Oops. Another lie.

'I mean, I wrote an email to Amina and now I'm just about to start my homework.' There. At least that's some of the truth.

'Okay, well dinner won't be far away now. We'll have it when your Dad brings Sammy and Tommy home from footy training, okay?'

'Okay,' I say with a smile.

She walks out of the room and I spin the swivel desk chair back around to look at the computer screen. Okay, new promise. No more lying to Grandma. From now.

CHAPTER FIVE

THE ART OF A TACKLE

The noise of Sammy and Tommy's Saturday morning cartoons blast through the house while I crunch down on my breakfast cereal. It's the weekend! The best time of the week. My little brothers are in the lounge room, wrestling in front of *Teen Titans* instead of actually watching it. Dad is in the front yard mowing and Grandma is out with her best friend Denise. They are shopping and going to see a movie. Grandma hates shopping but loves going to the movies. And she loves seeing Denise.

Jimmy, of course, is having his usual Saturday morning sleep in. He used to get up early like the rest of us but as soon as he became a teenager he started having weekend sleep-ins. I don't know how he can sleep with all this noise though—the cartoons have been turned up to the highest volume, Dad is mowing right outside his bedroom window and Sammy and Tommy keep yelling out what wrestling moves they are going to do to each other.

'It's time for some Sweet Chin Music,' Tommy roars.

I roll my eyes. They don't actually hit each other properly (Grandma would ground them so quickly) but they can go at it for hours.

And yet even with all that racket, Jimmy snoozes on. Normally I don't mind. I know Jimmy will always find time to hang out with me at some point in his weekend. But it is annoying me today because I am finally going to tell him about how I played rugby league on Wednesday. And I don't think I can wait any longer!

I didn't go back to the park on Thursday or yesterday because I walked home with Bethany and I promised Grandma I wouldn't dawdle. Plus my knees needed some time to heal. But I reckon I can do it again next Wednesday when Bethany has dancing. I'll just have to think of an excuse for Grandma.

Bethany was pretty proud of me for playing but she has zero interest in rugby league. And I don't think she liked the idea of how rough I made it sound.

'You should have seen me break Bobby Jones in half,' I said when I told her about it on the phone on Wednesday night.

'Mmm … I guess,' she replied. 'I'm glad you're chasing your dream, Dani, but you shouldn't 'break' someone.'

I've been thinking a lot about what she said though. Not about breaking Bobby, but about this being my dream. And this is why I need Jimmy to wake up. Because Bethany is right. I've had my first taste of footy in the park, but it's not enough. I want to be a Banford Saint too and now Jimmy is all part of my master plan. I'm going to ask him to help me get better at rugby league so I can prove to Grandma and Dad that I can play. I'm no longer just a super-secret spy, but also a secret genius. I slurp the rest of the milk out of my bowl and stare hard at Jimmy's bedroom door.

I want him to help me work on my tackling so I can be as good a fullback as Kalyn Ponga or James Tedesco or, even better, one of those girls in those photos on the Internet. I want to learn how to do the different types of kicks so I can be an even bigger threat on the field. And, most importantly, I want to learn how to catch the really big kicks so I don't make any more mistakes like I did last week.

Even though I was really proud of my tackle on Bobby, I can still sometimes hear how the boys laughed at me when I dropped that kick. I mean, the professional players do it all the time … But I guess I have to prove myself a little bit more than the boys do.

Suddenly, Jimmy's door opens. I can't believe my luck! It's 9am and he's already out of bed. His eyes look puffy and his dark hair is all pushed to one side, but he's awake.

'Jimmy!' I shout, leaping down from the kitchen stool.

I race to his side and start talking as fast as I can.

'Whoa, whoa, whoa, kiddo,' he says, putting his hand in my face. 'Halt. Stop. Enough. Let me at least open my eyes, okay?'

I poke my tongue out so he whips his hand away from my face in disgust.

'Blergh,' he says, wiping his hand on his shirt as I giggle.

'Well, can I make you breakfast? Will that help you wake up?' I ask.

'What's the rush, kiddo?' Jimmy laughs. 'You got something you need to talk about?' He browses the cereal boxes on the kitchen bench. Eyebrows arched in deep thought, he adds: 'If you're offering, I'll take a bowl of Nutri-Grain.'

'Coming right up!' I declare.

I run back into the kitchen and pull open the fridge door. I have practised my speech over and over and so I tell him about how I played rugby league in the park and how I want to be good enough so Dad and Grandma will let me play for the Banford Saints.

By the time I finish, Jimmy is chewing slowly on a mouthful of Nutri-Grain, a small frown across his face. I like the fact it's only small and also not a cranky frown. Maybe there's still a chance he'll agree to help me.

'So, what do you think?' I ask. I clasp my hands together and try to make my eyes looks big and sad. 'Can you help train me and make me the best player possible? Pretty please?' I hold my breath.

'Hmmm …' Jimmy sighs. He stares down into his bowl before looking out into the yard where Dad is finishing up the mowing. His pause is killing me.

'If I do this, we're going to do it my way,' he says, turning back to stare me straight in the eyes. He has hazel eyes, just like Dad and me. 'That means, we're going to start with tackling. I don't care if you want to be the fastest player or the one with the coolest step. I don't care if those boys laughed at you for dropping a ball. Knowing how to tackle properly is the most important starting point.'

I've never seen Jimmy look so serious so I do a big nod, making my bushy, hard-to-contain ponytail bounce, to let him know I'm ready.

'And I don't like keeping it a secret. I'm giving you one week to tell Dad what's going on. If you haven't told him by next Saturday, I won't help anymore … or I'll ask him to help instead.'

He raises his eyebrows at me in a challenge. Dad helping me?! No way!

I stick my hand out to Jimmy.

'Deal,' I say.

'Deal,' he says, grabbing my hand in return.

'When can we start?'

'Well,' Jimmy says, looking at the clock. 'The reason I'm already awake is because Dad needs me to watch you ratbags while he goes to help Aunty Bridget with her house renovations. If Tommy and Sammy agree to play in the backyard with us, maybe we can do it when he goes.'

Getting my twin brothers outdoors is never a problem. An hour later the four of us are in the backyard. Sammy and Tommy are in the treehouse and out of the way (thank goodness). I'm ready to go.

I have on some old shoulder pads I found in the garage, a massive t-shirt that Dad wears whenever he is doing work around the house (I needed something big enough to fit over the shoulder pads) and some Banford Saints footy shorts that Jimmy wore when he was younger. My feet are bare, my wild hair is tied back as good as I can get it and I've ripped off the band aids Grandma put on my knees. Only two scabs remain. It's show time.

Jimmy walks out of the house with an old headgear

and a tackling pad in his hands. He throws the headgear my way.

'Safety first,' he says. 'Okay, so today we'll start with tackling. Tomorrow I'll test you out under the high ball like you asked. At least Dad won't get suspicious tomorrow if we're just kicking and catching. But tackling is a lot more work.'

He hands me the tackling pad and steps back.

'Walk tall, stand proud, Murphy,' he says.

I straighten my shoulders and tighten my grip on the tackling pad.

'Now, the most important lessons to start with are these: hit with your shoulder first and aim for under the ball. Have your head on the opposite side of your shoulder, tucked against the side of the attacking player's hip. Wrap your arms and drive with your legs. Hold the pad and let me show you.'

Jimmy jogs forward and lightly tackles the bag. I immediately see the way he places himself to make a strong but safe tackle. It shows me that when I tackled Bobby the other day, I bent my head too far down.

'See that?' he asks. I nod, ponytail bouncing once again.

'Good,' he says. 'You must always protect your inside shoulder and the power and drive should come from your legs. To be safe, always keep your head and eyes up. When you lower or duck your head, you can get injured.'

Another nod.

'Now,' he says with a glint in his eye, 'hand me the pad, kiddo.'

For the next hour, I run and run and run at Jimmy's pad. I practise tackle after tackle after tackle—left shoulder, right shoulder, left shoulder, right shoulder. By the end, I may as well have not even worn the shoulder pads. My arms are aching and burning and I know they'll be red when I take my shirt off.

But, no matter how sore I am, I am really happy. Even Sammy and Tommy are impressed with how well I'd done and are chanting for me from the treehouse.

'Dani, Dani, Dani,' they call. I feel like a real footballer. Jimmy even made them swear they wouldn't tell Dad or Grandma until I did.

I feel like I've really accomplished something today. But I also think I'm going to need an afternoon nap.

***

'Dani,' Dad says as he walks into the kitchen, 'up for our usual Sunday morning run tomorrow?' He claps a hand on my shoulder as he walks past me to the fridge.

I wince as the pain shoots down my arm. I can barely

lift my spoon to my mouth to eat my delicious tomato soup. Jimmy worked me so hard. How will I be able to run tomorrow?

'Um,' I mutter, my legs screaming at me to say no, 'sure, Dad. Eight o'clock?'

'Eight o'clock,' he winks as he sits down at the end of the table, scattering grated cheese over the top of his soup.

My family always eats dinner together. It's our ritual and I love it. Another ritual is my Sunday morning run with Dad. Him and Jimmy always do morning runs during the week—really early, sometimes even when it's still dark! But on Sundays, Jimmy sleeps in and it's my turn to go out with Dad. So, even though I'm seriously sore, I'm not going to cancel on Dad.

'How was everyone's day?' Dad asks, slurping his soup into his mouth.

Grandma frowns at him and I have to stop myself from giggling. It is a pretty gross noise.

'It was good,' I say. I'm not ready to tell Dad that I did tackling practice with Jimmy. I know I'm supposed to as part of our deal, but maybe tomorrow … or maybe the day after that.

'The Roosters play the Sharks tonight, Dad. Are you going to watch?' I ask, trying to change the subject.

'Of course, I am. Can't miss my Chooks.'

Jimmy laughs.

'No way are they going to beat the Sharks tonight,' he says. 'You're dreaming. You have too many injuries.'

Dad rolls his eyes in a playful way as he and Jimmy break out into an argument. Or 'banter' as Dad likes to call it. Dad actually hates real arguments and never likes to be mad at us. That's why Grandma has to do a lot of the disciplining.

I watch Dad as he eats his soup. His eyes crinkle every time he smiles and his thongs slap his pale feet as he jiggles his leg. The rest of his legs are very tan, but his feet are super white because they're always hidden from the sun by his work boots.

'Are you going to watch tonight's game, Dani?' Dad asks me.

'I'll be there,' I say. 'I'll join the Roosters bandwagon for you, Dad. Boo the Sharkies!'

'That's my girl,' Dad chuckles.

'Can we watch?' Sammy and Tommy ask at the same time. It's creepy how often they do that.

'No,' Grandma says before Dad can reply. 'You know it's a 7:30pm bedtime for you, boys.'

'Ohhhh,' they groan.

'Maybe just the first half for them, Josie?' Dad suggests.

Josie, or Josephine, is Grandma's real name. Dad's

name is Leo. Mum's name was Jessica. Sammy looks at Grandma, his hands joined together like he's praying.

'Pretty please, Grandma?' Tommy asks.

'Oh, all right,' she sniffs, with a tiny smile on her face. 'But no complaining tomorrow if you're tired. And your Dad can put you two to bed. I have a date night with my television and Colin Firth.'

'Blergh,' Jimmy says, pretending to be sick hearing about Grandma's Hollywood crush. We all laugh together as the twins hi-five each other and Grandma smiles properly. I feel very warm and I don't think it's just because of my soup. I love my family. I just hope I don't disappoint Dad or Grandma when I finally share my life's greatest desire … my rugby league secret.

CHAPTER SIX

STEPHANIE ANNETTE HARDEN

'Ta-da!' Grandma exclaims, as she pulls a book out from behind her back.

I look at the cover and instantly recognise the bright colours, the image of two girls creeping behind a wall, a magnifying glass in the hands of one. It's the mystery book I have been eyeing off for months! 'Oh my goodness! Grandma! You bought it for me!'

'Yes, I saw it today and I knew you were saying you wanted to read it so I thought I'd grab it for you. Saves you from having to read the same old books over and over.'

She nods towards my shelves which are jampacked with books, some sadly falling apart. I love to read. So does Grandma. And even though I am 10, nearly 11, she still comes in to 'tuck me in' before bed every night so we can talk all about our books. It's one of our favourite things to do together.

'What did you think of the one from last week?' Grandma asks as she sits on the edge of my bed and nods towards another book on my bedside table.

'Ohhhh, I loved it,' I say. 'I think I like mysteries.'

Grandma smiles, but little does she know I am just like these detectives and spies I read about, still investigating my own mystery of the red-headed girl. I don't have any leads, but I will find out who she is. Just like a real detective would.

'I used to love mystery books too,' Grandma says as she smooths her light brown hair back into its bun.

'Really?'

'Yes. I used to love a book series called *The Famous Five*. Maybe you can give that a go when you're ready for something new.'

'That sounds good,' I smile. I love Grandma's book suggestions. She gives me a kiss on the forehead, stands up and turns my lamp on for me.

'Remember, Daniella, only half an hour of reading and then go to sleep. It's a Thursday and you have school in the morning,' she says.

As she walks towards my door, a thought occurs to me.

Grandma has always worked at home. She raised Mum while my Grandpa worked for a newspaper. He died only three months before Mum did so that's another reason why Grandma came and lived with us. She was alone too. Now she helps raise us. I think about what Bethany said about my playing rugby league being my 'dream'. I wonder if Grandma had a secret dream too when she was a little girl? Just like me?

'Hey Grandma,' I say as she reaches the door, my own thoughts escaping my mouth yet again. First Tyrone, now Grandma. It's like word vomit.

'Yes, Daniella?'

'Grandma, what was your dream?'

She stops. She was about to turn my main light off but her hand drops and she tilts her head.

'What do you mean?' she asks.

'I mean, did you always want to be a stay-at-home mum? Or did you have other dreams?'

She walks back to the bed, a slight frown on her face.

'Why do you ask?'

'I'm just being curious,' I shrug.

'Well, before I met your Grandpa, I did want to be a hairdresser. I used to love doing my friends' hair and my own too, of course.'

'Like how you like to do mine as well? And how you

used to do Mum's?'

Grandma smiles and I think I see her eyes go watery.

'Yes, Daniella, just like that. But, you know, I did always want to be a Mum. That was a dream of mine too and I was very lucky to have your Mum. It was my favourite job. Aside from being your Grandma, of course.'

She puts her finger to my nose and chuckles.

'Well, I'm glad you're my Grandma,' I say and then I pause. 'Do … do you think everyone should chase their dreams, no matter what?'

She tilts her head again and sighs. Her eyes scan my face.

'I fear this answer may come back to bite me on the bottom,' she says, squinting her eyes slightly at me. 'You should always chase your dreams. Why? What are your dreams?'

I'm still not ready to tell her. I don't know why. It seems like the perfect moment but I can't.

'I still don't know,' I say, shrugging. 'Maybe I could be a super-secret spy.'

Grandma laughs.

'With an imagination like that, you might be better off being the one who writes these books you love so much,' she says. 'It certainly seems safer.'

She scans my face for a moment and then runs one

finger under my chin, tracing the outline of my scar. Then she sighs, pats me on the hands, kisses me good night once again and leaves the room.

I touch my chin now and look down at my book sitting in my lap. I guess I can't call myself a very good super-secret spy until I solve the mystery of the red-haired girl. Maybe once I do that, I will tell Grandma my real dreams. I just need to solve my mystery.

***

The referee puts the whistle to his lips and the noise rings out across the grounds—it's game over. Everyone on the sideline claps and cheers as Jimmy and his teammates start their war cry to celebrate their 14-10 win. It's their first game of the season and I know Jimmy will be really happy with his team.

I look up at the bright lights that beam down on the field, my legs swing under my seat, and I watch the small clouds that come out of my mouth as I breathe upwards. Lots of teeny bugs fly around the lights. It's pretty cold on this Friday night so I'm really grateful that Jimmy had the earlier game and not the late kick-off.

But then, as I look down from the lights, I see who is running out onto the field for the second game of the night.

'It's her,' I whisper, leaping out of my seat.

Jimmy and his teammates have formed a guard of honour to cheer the under-12s onto the field. I had no idea the 12s were the second game of the night. But sure enough, there she is. She's wearing black headgear, but I can see her long, red hair poking out of the back, the tight braid swinging from side to side as she runs.

I race to the sideline. Jimmy will take ages to shower and get changed and then Dad always treats him to something from the canteen, so I know I should at least get to watch the first half. I press my body against the railing that borders the field and lean forward as far as I can.

A new referee takes to the field and blows his whistle, signalling the start of the game. The other side—the Green Hill Dolphins—kick off. The red-headed girl is a second rower, which makes sense to me given how tall and strong she looks. She takes the third run of the game and BOOM! She smashes past three defenders before finally someone drags her down. It's not a tackling style that Jimmy would approve of, but it does stop her.

The whole first half continues like that. She is the best runner in the Banford Saints' under-12s team by a long way. She doesn't score any tries or do anything fancy, but she easily makes the biggest impact.

It really is like watching a real-life version of Wonder

Woman—I feel like I'm actually in the movie, standing right next to her as she runs through a battle with everything just bouncing off her. Except the red-haired girl doesn't have a shield or the wrist cuffs. There's no lasso. It's all her.

'Daniella!' I hear Grandma call to me as the clock ticks closer to halftime. 'It's time to go home!'

I look over my shoulder.

'One more minute? Please?'

Grandma looks at the scoreboard. It's 12-all. She probably thinks I just want to see what happens. But really I've been struck with a new secret genius plan.

'Okay,' she nods. 'You have until halftime but then we're going.'

I turn back to the field. I must find out her name before I go. Every time she makes a run it sounds like people start cheering for 'Effie', but I need to know for sure.

It's super-secret spy time. Agent Murphy is a go.

I creep behind the people who stand along the sideline, my eyes switching between the field and the Banford Saints' bench.

'C'mon ref,' one man yells.

'Get them onside,' a Green Hill woman mutters.

'It's just the under-12s,' I hear the mother of a Banford

53

player say as she stares sideways at the Green Hill woman.

I finally reach the bench. The red-headed girl hasn't had a break all half but I'm hoping I hear the coach or another player say her name. Maybe I'll even have to interrogate someone.

But—aha!—even better. A trainer has the team sheet!

'Hey Alf,' the coach says to the trainer. 'I think Freddie has a busted nose.'

The trainer looks up from his clipboard and sees the halfback with blood streaming down his face. He puts the clipboard down, picks up a water bottle and races onto the field. I can't be seen. I can't be heard. I must be invisible. It's go time, Agent Murphy.

I tiptoe around the back of the Banford Saints' bench to where the clipboard lies on top of an esky. No one has noticed me. I snatch it up and turn my back to the bench (just in case). I scan down the list: No.7—Freddie Ward, No. 8—Jason MacPherson, No. 9—Kumail Rodini, No. 10—Lachlan Packer.

And then, No.11—Stephanie Annette Harden.

I have a name. They weren't calling out Effie. They were cheering for Stephie. The referee blows his whistle again to signal the end of the half and I watch as Stephanie walks to the dressing rooms with the team.

'Hey kid,' a trainer barks at me. I'm still holding on

tight to the clipboard, staring in awe at Stephanie. 'Can I have my stuff back?'

Oops, cover blown. Abort mission, Agent Murphy, abort mission.

I gulp and nod as I pass the clipboard back to the trainer, then I sprint to my family's car. I climb into the middle seat with Jimmy right behind me. It feels like I can hear my heart beating in my ears. I look up at Jimmy. I promised him I would tell Dad and Grandma what was happening within the week. It's Saturday again tomorrow.

Jimmy notices me staring at him and frowns slightly. I nod to him and turn to face the front of the car.

'Dad. Grandma,' I say loudly, 'I want to play rugby league for the Banford Saints.'

CHAPTER SEVEN

MISSION IMPOSSIBLE

To: soccer.star@mailbox.com

From: dani.number1@mailbox.com

Subject: HELPPPPP

Amina!! SOS! How did you get your Mum
and Dad to let you play soccer???

To: dani.number1@mailbox.com

From: soccer.star@mailbox.com

Subject: Uh oh

Hey to you too Dani! It was my Dad's
idea for me to play. He used to play back
in Iraq. Let me guess ... you're not
allowed to play rugby league?

To: soccer.star@mailbox.com

From: dani.number1@mailbox.com

Subject:Re: Uh oh

I finally told my Grandma and Dad on Friday night that I want to play. The whole car just went SUPER quiet and no one said anything (except stupid Tommy who kept giggling). Then when we got home my Dad came into my bedroom and just said he'll think about it. But we all know that means a big, fat, NO! No one has brought it up since. I swear the silence is WORSE than them being angry at me. It's been SO annoying. Jimmy is still doing some practise with me but Dad and Grandma are pretending like nothing happened and I've been too scared to bring it up again. I was so brave the first time. What do I do?!

To: dani.number1@mailbox.com

From: soccer.star@mailbox.com

Subject: Amina to the rescue!

I have an idea. When I wanted to get a dog but Mum and Dad said NO, I didn't give up. Do you hear me Dani? DO NOT GIVE UP. I proved to them how much I wanted a dog by getting those sticky Post-it

notes and putting one on the fridge each
day. Every day I would write a different
reason why I could look after a dog.
Like, I will take her to soccer practice
so she could go for runs. Things like
that! Now I have Daphne and I love her!
You should do that!

To: soccer.star@mailbox.com

From: dani.number1@mailbox.com

Subject: You're better than Sam Kerr!

You're brilliant!!! Thank you!!!
PS - Spider-Man is on Channel 10 on
Saturday! I know he's your favourite!
PPS - I had to Google Sam Kerr. I don't
know any famous soccer players. Now I do.
And you're cooler than her. And she seems
REALLY cool.

***

I pick off a chunk of my big chocolate Easter egg, shove
it in my mouth and stare at the fridge. After Amina's
amazing idea, I have left a message for Dad and Grandma
on the fridge every day for two whole weeks. That's
fourteen reasons why I should be allowed to play rugby
league. Number one? Because lots of girls play. Number
two? Because Jimmy has taught me how to tackle properly.
Number three? Because I could be really, really good.

Each morning I stick my reason to the fridge. By dinner time they are gone. I don't know who takes them down or where they go. I even tried to be a super-secret spy again on Sunday to watch where it went, but as soon as Jimmy asked me if I wanted to go play in the backyard, I forgot all about my mission and when I came back inside, my message was gone again (it was 'Number six: I could play for Australia one day!'). The detectives from my novels would be very disappointed in me.

Now I'm trying to think of reason number fifteen. I think about Grandma. While Dad said he'd 'think about it', Grandma has not spoken to me about it at all.

I feel sorry for Grandma sometimes because I think she misses my mum a lot. I know I do. But she says Mum was always her little girl. Sometimes when Grandma tries to tame my crazy hair, she tells me how Mum used to love having her hair done in fancy styles. I hate having my hair done. I can't sit still long enough. But I think Grandma wishes I did like it, just like Mum did.

She always says now that I'm her little girl and that she has to look after me. So maybe she's afraid I'll become too rough if I play rugby league?

'It's too rough and too dangerous … you're my little lady, not some kind of thug,' I hear her voice in the back of my head again.

That's definitely it. She thinks I will be too much like my brothers, too aggressive. Reason number fifteen has to be just for Grandma. I get up off the kitchen stool and put the rest of my Easter egg in the fridge before taking my marker out of my pocket.

Number fifteen, I write on my sticky note, *I won't become a thug.*

As I stick the note to the fridge, our home phone starts to ring. It's probably Bethany. Grandma, Dad and Jimmy all have mobile phones so no one ever rings our home phone except for Bethany and people who are trying to sell stuff.

'Hello, Daniella speaking?' I answer in my best polite voice, just the way Grandma taught me.

'Oh … uh, hey Dani,' a voice says from the other end.

I recognise who it is immediately. It's Tyrone Walker. I almost drop the phone in shock. Tyrone Walker has never called me. I don't even know if he knows my real name is Daniella.

'Tyrone?' I ask.

'Yeah, yeah it's me! How are your Easter holidays going?'

'Oh, good thanks. How are yours?'

'They're fine. A bit boring but I got loads of chocolate. Hey, listen, some of us boys were going to the park soon to play a game of footy and I wanted to see if you'd like to play? You were really good that day you came down but you haven't been back.'

This time I actually do drop the phone.

'Whoops, oh sorry Tyrone!' I squeal as I pick it back up. 'Yeah, I'd love to come play! Are you just going to Windemere Park?'

'Yep, that's it. Meet you there in 15 minutes?'

'Ok, see you soon. Thank you!'

I put the phone down and race into my bedroom to get out of my jeans and into some shorts. I grab my joggers out of the cupboard and some socks out of my drawers and race into Dad's bedroom. He's sitting on the bed reading his Kindle.

'Hey Dad, do you mind if I go to the park to play for a bit?'

Dad looks up from his book and frowns slightly. He gets Easter time off from work, just like us kids.

'Who else is going?'

'Oh … just some kids from my grade. You know Tyrone Walker?'

Dad nods slowly.

'Mmm … is Bethany going?'

'If she is, can I go?'

'Yes,' Dad says. 'But only for an hour. I'm making a

roast for lunch so I'd like you to be home for that, please.'

'With sweet potatoes?' I ask.

'Do you really think I'd forget sweet potatoes?'

'Our favourite?' I ask with a grin. 'Never!'

He smiles.

'Off you go, Dani.'

I race back to the kitchen to call Bethany, who luckily answers on the second ring.

'Bethany!' I exclaim.

'Dani! How are you? You sound like you've eaten too much chocolate.' Bethany laughs her high-pitched laugh.

'Oh my gosh Beth, you won't believe what's just happened!' I look around the kitchen to make sure no one is nearby to overhear my conversation. 'Tyrone Walker just called and asked me to go to the park with him to play rugby league!'

Bethany gasps loudly.

'Daniella,' she says, 'please tell me you're going.'

'We-ell … I can only go if you go. I told Dad I was going to play with you.'

It's silent on the other end. Bethany and I hardly ever break the rules. Mitch Delaney calls us the 'goody-two-shoes duo' of Mrs Crawley's class. Whatever that means. But, I have to say, Bethany is an angel. I can tell Dad and Grandma little white lies and only feel a teeny bit guilty.

Bethany never even dares to lie.

'I … I don't know, Dani,' she says.

'We can play though,' I say. 'We'll go on the swings and can play some hopscotch. It's not lying. We just won't tell anyone I'm also playing rugby league down there.'

'Mmmm … I guess so. Promise me we'll play?'

'Of course! I haven't seen my best friend all Easter holidays. I definitely want to play with you too.'

'Okay then. I'll just go ask my mum.'

Two minutes later, Bethany has the tick of approval from her mum and I'm racing out the door. I want to sprint off to the park but I'll need all my energy for the game so I walk as calmly as possible. It's pretty cool that Tyrone thought to invite me. I'm beginning to feel like one of the boys. Or, better yet, I'm beginning to feel like Stephanie Annette Harden. One of the girls.

When I get to the park, Bethany looks just as excited as me. It seems all her worries are gone, but that's why she's my best friend. She'd do anything I ask her to, and I'd do the same for her. We've been best friends since we were five.

'Oh my gosh Dani!' Bethany squeals as I sit down to put my shoes and socks on. 'This is so cool. I can't believe Tyrone invited you to play! I can't wait to see how you go!'

I look up at her, covering my eyes from the sun behind her blonde head, and smile.

'I'm so glad you were allowed to come play,' I giggle. 'Bethany, I'm going to score a try today and it's going to be for you. My best friend forever! We'll go on the swings as soon as the game is over.'

As I'm lacing up my joggers, Tyrone comes over and Bethany goes bright red.

'Oh, hey Bethany,' Tyrone says, his blue eyes going wide. 'I didn't know you were coming down.'

'Yep,' she says proudly. 'I have to see my best bud in action!'

'Well, she's really good. I think you'll be impressed.'

I feel my palms start to get a bit sweaty. It's like I have to be as good as an actual NRL player the way everyone is talking about me. It's making me feel nervous. I breathe in and out and just try to remember everything Jimmy has taught me.

'Um, so Dani,' Tyrone says, getting his mind back on the game. I should have warned him Bethany was coming. 'We're going to do the same teams as last time. You happy to be on the wing?'

'Yep!' I say.

'Okay, sweet. Five minutes until kick off.'

Tyrone turns and jogs back to the rest of the boys. I notice he's running with his back a little straighter. He looks a little taller. I giggle.

'I think someone is trying to impress you,' I say to Bethany.

'Oh, be quiet Daniella Murphy,' Bethany says, pretending to hit out at me. But then when she thinks I'm not looking, she smooths down her hair. I think she's trying to impress Tyrone too.

I start stretching on the ground and Bethany sits down next to me, picking at the grass while staring off into the distance.

'Bethany, you're going to make me vomit,' I whisper.

'What?! Why?!'

'You should be here to watch me,' I giggle. 'Not Tyrone!'

'Oh, you really are the worst,' she laughs. 'You know I am here to watch you. I'm your best cheerleader, Dani. See?'

She starts joining me in stretching and I laugh.

'I know,' I say. 'I know you hate lying to your mum so I'm really happy you agreed to come.'

'I can be a bad kid when I want,' she grins.

'It's game time, team,' Tyrone calls out across the park.

'Okay,' I say, standing up and wiping the grass off my hands. 'Wish me luck!'

'Good luck,' Bethany says. 'Kick their butts!'

I smile as I jog onto the field. I certainly plan on kicking some butts today.

CHAPTER EIGHT

GAME ON

'Go, Dani!' Bethany yells from our imaginary sideline as I take my place on the wing.

I pick up a blade of grass and throw it into the wind like I've seen some footballers do on TV. It's a pretty breezy day and we're kicking into the wind, so it could be a bit tough for us. I look up at the sky, which has a lot of grey clouds scattered across it today. It gives me a little shiver.

As I look back down, I realise the game is about to start. Tyrone looks to his left and then his right to make sure we're all onside before kicking off. Tingles shoot through my body, just like they did on the night I first saw Stephanie Annette Harden. As Tyrone's boot hits the ball, I want to scream out in excitement.

My team runs forward as the kick goes high before landing nicely in the arms of Harry Marshall. He passes it off to big Micah Carroll who runs straight down the middle. He's tackled and the play goes on.

'C'mon Dani!' Bethany calls out. 'Go get 'em!'

I hear Mitch Delaney laugh at what Bethany says and I roll my eyes. Pest. I thought I had proven so much but clearly it's not enough.

The play goes back and forth a little bit but I don't really get the chance to do much. I notice Bethany's gone a bit quieter on the sideline and I hope she's not bored already. She did me a huge favour coming down here today, so I have to make it worth it for her. I just need the opportunity to do another big tackle, like I did in my first game with these boys. Or maybe score a try. I've never done that before.

Mitch Delaney's team gets the ball again, so I know my chance must be coming for a big hit.

'Third tackle,' Simon Butler, our 'referee', yells out.

Harry goes into hooker and passes the ball out to his centre, Sione Tasi, who barges forward. He's a big guy, but I reckon I can handle him.

Both me and my centre, Jordan Hockings, run forward to try to bring Sione down but I get there first. I try to remember everything Jimmy taught me but I'm also thinking about how I have to impress Bethany and prove Mitch wrong. As I bend down to make my tackle, I know instantly I've done something wrong.

I've hit with my shoulder first, just like Jimmy showed me. I've wrapped my arms around Sione and I'm pushing with my legs, just like Jimmy said. But, as I start to make contact, I realise far too late that my head is in the wrong place. It's only for a second, but it feels like my heart is in my throat as I see what's about to happen. And then—

Bang! My head smacks into Sione's chest. Everything hurts and I'm falling backwards. My body hits the ground and it seems like everything is upside down. I hear Tyrone yell out and I hear Bethany scream. I can taste blood and I can smell dirt. I try to speak but it's like my brain and mouth aren't working together anymore. I see the blue sky above … I see some dark spots and then …

Then everything goes black.

CHAPTER NINE

KNOCKED OUT

I open my eyes to white. Everything is white. The ceiling above me, the sheets that cover me, the walls around me, the rails on the bed … my Dad's face. *My Dad.* Uh-oh. I stare into his eyes for a few moments before everything starts coming back to me.

I don't remember much about being at the park except that after everything went black I woke up to Bethany crying over me while a bald man who I've never seen before did some tests and asked me some questions. I tried to reply when he asked me what day it is (Tuesday! It's Tuesday!) but I couldn't.

Then I remember seeing that man again in the back of a van. I remember hearing sirens. I remember feeling scared and sick in my tummy.

Now, I'm here. Looking at Dad. He looks old today.

'Daniella,' he says as we stare at each other. His voice is croaky like when he's just woken up in the morning.

'Daniella!' a shrill voice squawks to my left, sending shivers down my body. I look over as Grandma stands up and grabs my hand. 'How do you feel? Are you okay?!'

I look at her and then look to my right. Jimmy is sitting there, elbows on his knees, his head bent down. He's scrunched his thick, dark hair into his hands. I can't see his face but I see some tears drop onto the hospital floor. I know where I am now. I know what's happened. And I know what's about to happen.

I'm in so much trouble. I look back at Dad.

'D-Dad?' I stutter. My mouth feels dry. Grandma knows straight away what I want and hands me a paper cup of water before sitting back down. She drags her seat closer to the bed.

'Daniella,' he says, standing up taller at the end of my bed. 'You've suffered a pretty bad concussion but the doctor thinks you're going to be okay.'

My head suddenly pounds. It's like it has its own heartbeat.

'She said you could have some memory loss, dizziness, headaches, and feel sick or tired. But once she sees you,

you'll get to come home. You also bit your tongue and there was a little bit of bleeding, but nothing too bad. So now, my first question is, how do you feel?'

I gulp.

'Um … okay. My head does hurt a bit.' I bite my lip.

'Ok, well they might be able to give you some medicine for that. Now. My second question.'

I grip my fingers around the hospital sheets. I feel like pulling them up over my head and disappearing forever.

'Daniella Grace Murphy, what on earth were you doing with Bethany to suffer a concussion in the first place?'

I look at Jimmy. I've never seen Dad like this and I suspect he already knows what I was doing. I bet Bethany already told him. I can't blame her. I remember her scream and I remember her crying. She's probably so scared right now. She might be in trouble too and it's all my fault. Jimmy looks up at me and he is no longer crying but he looks serious. He gives me one nod, so I look back at Dad. No more lying. I promised.

'I was at the park with Bethany, that's not a lie, but I was mainly there to play rugby league with Tyrone and some other kids from school,' I say, looking at my hands. I can still see some dirt on them from the park, even under my fingernails. I hope I haven't made a mess of these white sheets. 'I was trying to make a tackle on Sione but I put my head in the wrong place and … well, that's kind of all I remember.'

I look back up at the room. Dad looks the maddest I have ever seen him look. Jimmy is staring at the floor again. He must already be in trouble. And Grandma is sitting in her chair, her lips tight. She's gripping her little purple handbag. It's weird. Normally Grandma is the one with a lot to say and Dad is the quiet one. It's making me nervous, but I can smell Grandma's lavender from where I lie, and it gives me the smallest bit of comfort. I turn back to Dad.

'I wasn't trying to be naughty, Daddy, I promise,' I say, my stomach churning. My throat feels sore just from trying to force the words out. 'I just want to play rugby league. I want to play like Jimmy and Sammy and Tommy. I want to play for the Banford Saints.' I feel hot all over and I know the tears are starting to bubble up inside of me. 'I … I don't want to be treated differently to my brothers. And I know you said you'd think about whether I could play with the Saints but I didn't think that meant I couldn't play with my friends.' I scrunch my face up hard to stop the tears from spilling out. I just have to get my message out. 'I've only done it two times but Jimmy has been training me too and he's done a really good job!'

There. Everything I've wanted to say finally bursts out of me. The whole truth. I found my voice. But judging by Dad's face, it hasn't done me any good.

'Daniella,' Dad says, 'you could have been seriously injured. You never asked permission to play rugby league at the park so I don't know why you would presume it would just be okay. It's not okay. You know we wouldn't have allowed it.'

'But Dad!' I lurch forward, my head pounding harder. 'It's not fair. The boys can play whenever they want to. Why can't I?'

Dad begins to shake his head but it's Grandma who finally speaks up.

'You are a little girl, Daniella!' she exclaims. I turn to look at her. I've never heard her voice like this. It's really high and squeaky. Grandma is the most beautiful woman I know and she never leaves the house without her hair and makeup done. Now as I look at her, I realise her hair is all loose in its bun and she doesn't have her usual lipstick on.

She reaches into her purse and pulls out a blue sticky note. It's my blue sticky note. The one I wrote before I went to the park.

Number fifteen: I won't become a thug.

'It's not because I am afraid you'll become a thug, Daniella,' she says with tears in her eyes. 'I don't want you to play because I am afraid you are going to get hurt. And I was right! Look at you! You are our little girl. You should not be in a hospital bed. I don't want to see you sick or hurt. We have already lost one of our girls. We can't lose another!'

I open my mouth ready to argue back but at the same time tears burn my eyes again. It all hits me. I look at Dad whose head is now down. One of our girls. This is about Mum. They don't want to lose me like they lost her. I feel silly and sad. My fingers find their way to the scar under my chin. It all makes sense now. But I didn't want to hurt anyone's feelings or scare anyone. And I'm not sick. I just want to play a game. I never even got to show them how good I could be.

'I'm sorry, Dani,' Dad says from the bottom of my bed. His voice is croaky as he lifts his head. 'Grandma is right. It's not safe. I can't risk it. You can't play for the Banford Saints. You can't play with your friends in the park. You can't train with Jimmy. I don't want to see or hear of you playing rugby league at all.'

'But Dad! She's really good!' Jimmy says, jumping out of his seat. 'And the exact same thing could happen to me or Sammy or Tommy. You guys have to give her a chance. You have to see what she can do. Today was a mistake. But she can play. She can tackle. I promise!'

I look back at Dad, hopeful that Jimmy's reaction will change his mind.

'No,' Dad turns to him. 'That is enough.'

He looks back at me, shaking his head.

'My word is final.'

CHAPTER TEN

GROUNDED

My name is Daniella Murphy and I am not a rugby league player. I am not a super-secret spy. I am just grounded. Well, for three months I am anyway. One month is almost down, but there's another two to go.

I'm sitting in Dad's ute with my homework in lap, staring out at the Banford Saints rugby league grounds.

I can see the ginormous gum tree that stands behind the goalposts. I can see a bunch of kids racing about, playing hide and seek. I can see some parents standing in a huddle near the canteen and the rather big man with the white moustache barking orders at his players on the field. They all get down on their backs and bend their legs and start doing sit ups. One boy counts as they go.

There is noise all around me, but I can't hear it because I'm trapped in Dad's car.

I still feel sad. It's been almost one whole month since I was in hospital. That's almost one whole month of being grounded. One whole month of doing Tommy and Sammy's share of chores. One whole month of trying to be the bestest friend ever to Bethany after she got in trouble for lying for me.

But, most importantly, it's been almost one whole month of knowing I will never play rugby league again. It sucks. It's been one whole month of sadness. Dad calls it 'sulking' but he doesn't understand. I really believed I was going to be a rugby league player. Now I don't know what to believe in. I don't even care about the maths homework that sits in my lap. Maths! My favourite subject!

I can see Stephanie Annette Harden from where I sit and that hurts even more. When I was banned from playing rugby league, I also gave up my secret identity as Agent Murphy. I don't know anything about Stephanie still except her name. Everything else is to remain a mystery. I sigh and put my head back against the car seat.

'Don't start with me, Daniella,' Dad says. He's reading his Kindle while we wait for Jimmy to finish training. Jimmy is also in a little bit of trouble. But his grounding ends on Thursday—only one month. I got three! Three months! I did lie way more than Jimmy though.

'But I didn't say anything,' I mumble back.

He looks over at me with his eyebrows raised and a slight smile.

'Good,' he says. 'Let's keep it that way then, hey? I didn't know if coming here tonight would inspire another speech from you.'

He ruffles my hair and turns back to his book. I gave up arguing with Dad about two weeks ago. His word really was final. Dad is normally a bit of a pushover, but this time around he's been really tough. I haven't been allowed out to play with Bethany, I haven't been allowed to use my email to talk to Amina (I really hope she doesn't think I'm ignoring her), I haven't even been allowed to walk home after school. Grandma picks me up now.

This must be what jail feels like. I hear the back door open. Jimmy jumps in the car, smelling of mud, letting in a woosh of cold air. Autumn is almost over.

'Hey kiddo, hey Dad,' he says. 'How was school today, Dani?'

'Fine,' I mumble.

'Whoa, slow down kid,' he says. 'Don't give me too much info at once. But seriously, what did you do today? What are you learning about at the moment?'

'Not much,' I say, feeling myself getting cranky with

Jimmy. I'm never normally cranky at Jimmy but I can't help it lately. I hate not being a boy like him. 'It was our library day. We did some division work in maths. Like I said, just the same as any other day.'

I hear Jimmy slump back in his seat.

'Okay then,' he says.

He quickly changes the subject and starts talking to Dad about some show they watch with kings and queens and boring war fights. I fiddle with the window switch. I know one day I'll get over it. Maybe in another two months when I'm not grounded anymore.

*****

I'm stacking the dishwasher after Thursday night dinner when Jimmy walks into the kitchen. Tommy and Sammy are flicking their peas at me from the kitchen table. Grandma says they can't leave until they've finished their whole dinner, but she went to the bathroom and now they've turned their food into a game.

'Head shot!' Tommy exclaims as a pea hits my cheek. 'Fifty points!'

'Booo, I only got her arm. That's just twenty,' says Sammy.

Jimmy walks over and yanks the forks out of their hands.

'That's enough,' he says.

'You can't tell us what to do!' whines Sammy.

'Well, do you want me to get Grandma instead?'

Tommy and Sammy look at each other, grin their evil little smiles and run from the table. Jimmy clears their plates and brings them to me at the dishwasher.

'So, you going to watch the Broncos with me tonight? They're playing the Bulldogs,' Jimmy says.

I frown at him.

'I can't,' I reply.

'That wasn't a rule of your grounding though, Dani,' Jimmy says. 'You can still watch rugby league.'

He's right. But I haven't been able to watch any games since I was banned from ever playing. It hurts too much. And I especially don't want to watch with Jimmy today. He's no longer grounded as of this afternoon. I feel guilty for how I'm treating him but I'm not allowed to be angry at Dad and Grandma. They'll just ground me longer. So, I'm angry at Jimmy instead.

'I just don't want to,' I reply, closing the door to the dishwasher.

'You know,' he says as he folds his arms, starting to sound a little angry himself, 'I didn't do anything wrong, Dani. It's not my fault they won't let you play anymore. I got in trouble too. I have only ever tried to help you.'

'You don't know what it's like!' I yell at him. He looks

shocked. I hardly ever yell. It's my word vomit again. 'You're allowed to play. Tommy and Sammy are allowed to play and they're younger than me! It's not fair. No one ever says no to you, Jimmy. No one ever says you can't do something because you're a boy. I just don't care about it anymore, okay? I don't care about the Broncos, I don't care about rugby league, I don't want to watch it.'

Jimmy's arms drop by his side. He looks at me with sad eyes but nods.

'Okay,' he says. 'But kiddo, you haven't been yourself for a while and I'm worried. If you need to be angry at me for a little bit longer, then fine. Whatever. I don't like it but I'll let it slide. But if you need to talk to someone, my room is right there.'

He points to his bedroom door.

'I wanted to help you play,' he says. 'I'm sorry we failed. But, walk tall, stand proud, Murphy. I promise you I will help you chase any other dream that you have. That's what big brothers do.'

I look up at him, just as Dad calls out to let us know the game is starting.

'That was my only dream,' I say.

CHAPTER ELEVEN

DON'T GIVE UP

I hear the whispering before I see them. You don't even need to be a super-secret spy to know Dad and Grandma are up to something. It's a Sunday night, now two months since I was grounded (only one month to go!) and I've just had my shower. I'm walking down the hallway and can hear Dad and Grandma in the kitchen.

'Hopefully this does the trick,' I hear Grandma whisper, although not very quietly.

'I don't think she'll go for it, but we have to try,' Dad replies.

I walk around the corner to find both of them sitting at the kitchen table. It feels like I've stumbled into a very important business meeting. I tug at the sleeve of my pyjamas, fresh from the dryer to help make me warm on this super chilly night.

'What are you two doing?' I ask.

'Oh, Daniella,' Grandma says, jumping slightly. 'We were actually waiting for you. Can you come and sit with us, please?'

My tummy is alive with butterflies. Dare I hope? Are they going to let me play rugby league? I quickly walk over and sit down with them. I put my hands on the kitchen table and clasp them together.

'We've been talking about this rugby league stuff and we want to meet you halfway,' Dad says. 'So, what if we find another sport for you to play, like netball?'

My hands squeeze together tighter as my body seems to turn cold. All the hope is gone.

'Why? Because netball is all girls can play?'

'Daniella!' Grandma exclaims, looking shocked. 'Do not speak back to your father like that.'

I sigh as Dad raises his eyebrows at me. It looked like he was actually almost about to smile, but if he was, it's already vanished.

I actually think netballers are amazing. We had some Queensland Firebirds players visit our school last year. But it's not the sport for me.

'I'm sorry, but no,' I reply more calmly.

'Ok, well, I'll try again. What about touch football?' Dad asks.

'No. No, thank you,' I say, feeling my jaw go tight as I force my words out through clenched teeth. 'I want to tackle.'

Now it's Dad's turn to sigh.

'Well, have a think and let us know if there's another sport you want to play because rugby league is not an option,' he says, getting up to leave.

'Rugby union?' I ask.

He looks back at me. 'Don't be smart, Daniella.'

Grandma looks at me sadly and follows Dad out of the room. I let my hands go from each other and slump slightly in my chair. I don't want to play any other sport. I want to play rugby league, but it really does feel like it's never going to happen.

'It might be time to give up, Dani,' I whisper to myself. I don't know what else I can do to make Dad and Grandma see. I think my dreams might be all over.

***

'Okay, Dani,' Mrs Crawley says. 'Spell ambulance.'

I hear someone giggle behind me. It's our Monday spelling bee at school.

'A-M-B-U-L-A-N-C-E,' I reply.

'Very good,' Mrs Crawley says.

As she turns her attention to the next student, I whip

my head around to see who giggled at me. Of course, it's Mitch Delaney. I bet he's thinking about that day at the park. Every time he sees me at school, he falls to the ground and pretends to be knocked out. Now he's staring at me, a wicked smirk on his face. He pokes his tongue out at me before doing a rude signal with his finger.

I turn back to the front.

'Excuse me, Mitchell Delaney,' Mrs Crawley says. Uh-oh. Busted. 'What were you just doing?'

'Nothing, Miss,' he says. 'I was just flicking my fingers.'

'Miss Murphy? Is that what just happened?'

I look at Mrs Crawley before turning to Mitch. He narrows his eyes at me as if it's a warning. I look back at the teacher.

'I didn't see what he did,' I lie. I'm no tattle.

Mrs Crawley's nostrils flare as she stares down at me.

'Mmmm-hmmm. Well then, Mr Delaney, can you please spell punishment?'

Now other kids are giggling at him.

'P-U-N-I-S-H-M-E-A-N-T?'

'There's no a in punishment, but fair try,' Mrs Crawley says. 'You'll have to do another word.'

She looks down at her list but Mitch butts in.

'While you're choosing a word for me, Miss, maybe

you can find another one for Dani too. Like embarrassing or weakling or sook?'

'Oooohhhh,' rings out around the classroom as I whip back around to stare Mitch in the face.

'Why don't you just shut up, Mitch Delaney,' I snap. 'The only weakling around here is you and the fact you're afraid I could snap you in half if I wanted to.'

A second, louder round of 'ohhhhh' vibrates around the room, mingled with laughter, as Mrs Crawley calls for quiet and Mitch turns a nasty shade of red. His face gets even pointier somehow and his eyes are so angry and narrowed, I can barely see the white of his eyeballs anymore.

'That is enough,' Mrs Crawley says loudly and firmly. 'Mr Delaney, Miss Murphy. You are both out of line. Mitchell, you are not to call your classmates names nor interrupt me while I am speaking. Daniella, while your outburst was very out of character for you, you are not to tell people to 'shut up' nor incite violence in the classroom!'

My hand shoots into the air. Mrs Crawley sighs.

'Yes, Dani?'

'I am sorry, Mrs Crawley. I wasn't trying to incite violence though. I was talking about a rugby league tackle,' I say quietly.

'I do not care,' she says. 'This is not the place to talk

about tackling either. Both of you will have lunchtime detentions with me.'

'But Miss!' Mitch goes to protest.

'No buts! Now, back to our spelling work.'

Mrs Crawley turns her attention to Cara Sanders, and I turn my attention to the window. I sigh. It's such a beautiful winter's day outside. The sun is shining really brightly, which means it's not too cold at all. The sky is my favourite shade of blue without even a spot of a white cloud and there's a small breeze rustling the trees on the back oval. It's like the trees are waving to me, taunting me that I don't get to be outside for my lunch.

I sigh, turn back to the front and fidget with my pen. I am furious with Mitch but I'm also really embarrassed by my outburst. I've been speaking my mind a lot more lately and while I actually like that I'm doing that, I have never been in trouble at school before.

I sneak a peek over at Bethany who is already looking at me. She pulls a sad face and shrugs her shoulders.

'Sorry,' she mouths to me.

I shrug back at her. I really am lucky to have her as my best friend. She was grounded for a week after the park incident but didn't even get mad at me. I bought her an ice cream from the school tuckshop with my pocket money as a thank you. She could have been furious with me. Instead, she's just listened to all my whinging and now this. She'll have to find someone else to play with at lunchtime because I lost my temper.

I just can't help it. Mitch Delaney is so rude and thinks he is so much better than me when he's not. He makes me so mad with the way he treats me, just because I'm a girl. It seems to be happening a lot lately in my life and I've had enough.

I peek up at the front of the classroom where Mrs Crawley is writing on the board. I quickly use the opportunity to spin around and glare at Mitch one last time. His head is down and he has his hair bunched in his hands so he doesn't see me.

But that's fine. I'll be sure to get my revenge later.

*****

The bell rings for lunch. Or, in the case of Mitch Delaney and I, it rings for detention.

As the rest of grade five rushes out of the doors towards freedom, Mitch and I sit at our desks waiting to hear what Mrs Crawley wants us to do.

'Okay folks,' she says, walking in front of her own desk and clasping her hands in front of her dress. 'Welcome to detention. Now, I have to quickly duck to the staff room to bring my lunch back here. You are welcome to get your own lunch to eat at your desk. But the task I want you to do today is to discuss between yourselves what your differences are and how you can overcome them. You must tell me your answer at the end of the lunch break.'

'What is this, *The Breakfast Club*?' Mitch snorts.

I frown at him. What on earth is he talking about?

'Very funny, Mr Delaney,' Mrs Crawley says. 'Although I am impressed by your apparent knowledge of movies from the 1980s. I'll be right back. Get to work, please.'

She walks out of the room. Mitch sighs and walks over to his bag to get his lunch out.

'What was that about?' I ask.

'What was what?'

'*The Breakfast Club*?'

'It's an old movie,' he says, shrugging his shoulders. 'My older sister showed me.'

He sits down at the desk next to me and pulls out a ham and cheese sandwich. I grimace—ham! Yuck!—then go get my lunch.

'Okay,' I say as I pull out my chicken sandwich and flip to a new page in my notebook. 'Let's get this over with. What are our differences?'

Mitch shrugs again.

'You like ham and I don't?' I offer with a smile. He rolls his eyes.

'Are you going to be any help at all?' I sigh.

'Well, this is stupid. We shouldn't even be in here. It's not like I called you any particularly bad words.'

'Yeah, well, you did make fun of me and I'm sick of it,' I reply. 'Oh wait, there's one difference. You're mean and I'm not.'

Mitch rolls his eyes again.

'You should see a doctor about your eye condition,' I say with another smile.

'Ha,' he snaps. 'I may be mean, but you're stuck up.'

'I am not!'

'Yeah, you are,' he says. 'People may think you're quiet and shy and sweet, but you don't fool me. You have a smirk. You get it whenever you answer a maths question correctly or whenever you win a race in P.E. You just did it then with your little jokes. We all know you're smart and fast. It's clear you know it too.'

I cross my arms across my chest. I feel like I've been slapped across the face. I smirk?!

'Coming from the biggest boaster in the whole school,' I say, my temper rising. 'Maybe that's a similarity between us.'

Mitch smiles down at his shoes, chewing on his sandwich.

'Maybe it is,' is all he says.

'You are so annoying, Mitch Delaney. Why do you pick on me so much? Why do you pick on everyone so much?!'

He looks up at me, chewing slowly. It looks like he's actually thinking hard about something.

'Do you really want to know?' he asks.

'Yeah, I do. But as if you'd tell the truth.'

He shrugs, starting to look as annoyed as I feel. 'I can tell the truth. But why should I tell you?'

'So we can get out of here? So we don't have to spend any more time together?'

'Oh, is it really that hard for you to be around me?' he shoots back. 'Well, if you must know, it's just ... well, it's just because I want to be the best. That's why I pick on everyone so much, as you say.'

I slump back in my chair. I can tell he's telling the truth. He's not lying or trying to be funny. I don't think he's even about to turn it into something mean.

'What do you mean?' I ask, all the anger and annoyance gone from my voice.

He huffs and puts down his sandwich.

'My dad expects me to the best at everything, just like my big sister is,' he says with a long sigh. 'She's the smartest, so I should be the smartest. But I'm not. She's the fastest swimmer at her high school, so I should be the fastest at something too. I'm good at running but I'm not the fastest. You're faster than I am. It annoys me. It's really hard to be the best at stuff. I didn't want you to play rugby league because … '

He trails off and stares at the ground again. There's a silence. I can tell he's wanted to tell someone this for a long time. I glance up and see Mrs Crawley standing quietly in the hallway. She must have heard him. It's like she's afraid to come in.

'Go on,' I say. 'I'm not going to make fun of you.'

'Well … I didn't want you to play rugby league because … because I didn't want you to be better than me,' he says, unable to look at me. 'It's the one thing I'm really good at. My only true competition is Tyrone. It's the one thing about me that seems to make my dad happy. But I know you're faster than me and I thought if you played, well I thought you might be better than me at that too. And I didn't want my dad to see that.'

Mitch sits there now picking at a bit of cheese that sticks out from his sandwich. I realise my own sandwich is sitting on the desk with a fly on top of it. Ew. My hands are sweaty and I can barely hold the pen. Double ew.

'Oh. Well, if it makes you feel better, I'm banned from playing rugby league ever again anyway.'

'What?!' Mitch says, suddenly looking up. His eyes

seem alarmed.

'Yeah. After I got knocked out, Dad and Grandma said I can never play ever again.'

'So?' Mitch asks.

'So? So what?'

'Well, is that really going to stop you?'

'They banned me! Didn't you hear what I said?'

Mitch shrugs again, finally turning his attention back to his sandwich.

'Look, I know what I said,' he says. 'I don't want you to be better than me. But Dani, you're good. You shouldn't give up just because someone tells you to.'

I look around the classroom quickly. I feel like this is all a big prank. This is not the Mitch Delaney I know.

'Why do you like rugby league so much anyway?' he asks. 'Why did you get into it?'

I smile and it's definitely not a smirk. This is one of my favourite stories.

'I just remember one night when I was almost five I couldn't go to sleep and I came out to the lounge room and my dad and my big brother were watching a Broncos and Cowboys game,' I say as I look down at my hands. 'It was a close game so they were shouting heaps and it seemed so exciting. Then Andrew McCullough scored a try to win the game and yeah … I don't know. I liked watching with them and cheering with them. My mum was there too and she made us popcorn and kept laughing at how excited we were while also pretending to care. It wasn't long before she died. It was fun. I just fell in love with the game from there and I always wished I could play it too.'

I finally look up at Mitch and he's half smiling.

'Then definitely don't give up,' he says.

I smile back. It's exactly what I needed to hear after last night's talk with Dad and Grandma.

'Also, you're becoming sassy lately. Keep that up.'

I laugh.

'Yeah, I think I'm just finding my voice.'

'Cool,' Mitch says with a dorky smile.

I smile back and then we quickly look away from each other. I feel a bit embarrassed but it was nice to get to know another side of Mitch.

'Anyway, what should we tell Mrs Crawley?' I ask, changing the subject. 'Maybe that we're not really all that different, we're just competitive and we need to work together instead of trying to always beat each other?'

He laughs.

'That actually sounds really good. I've done a few of these detentions now and Mrs Crawley will love that. You just have to suck up to the teacher and they let you go.'

I see Mrs Crawley cover her mouth to stop herself laughing in the hallway.

'Hey, Dani?' Mitch says.

'Yeah?'

'If you tell anyone what I said today, I'll make sure Bobby always kicks off towards you in the future.'

I smile, a little giggle escaping. In a weird way, I feel better than I have in weeks.

'Okay. You have a deal. And Mitch?'

'Yeah?' he says with a mouthful of ham, cheese and bread.

'Be nicer to everyone.'

He lets out a single laugh.

'Okay.'

CHAPTER TWELVE

STATE OF ORIGIN ...
WITH A TWIST

My eyes snap open. There is something in my room.

No! Wait! There is something outside my room. Just outside my door. I can hear it, rustling around. I sit up tall in my bed, my doona falling off me, my back as straight as a pole, my eyes wide, the hairs on the back of my neck tingling with anticipation. Something is out there. Or someone is out there. I'm afraid to move but I'm buzzing with energy all at once. I need to do something and instantly I know what.

It's time to bring Agent Murphy out of retirement. I try to get my eyes to adjust to the darkness of my bedroom.

My brain feels fuzzy from sleep but I need to focus. What clues do I have?

Aside from the rustling noise, I can make out a light dancing around through the crack under my door. It looks like a torch light or a light off someone's phone. Only three people in this house have a mobile phone—Grandma, Dad and Jimmy. But ... what if it's someone who doesn't live inside this house?!

I slowly move my legs to the right side of my bed and slip down to the ground. My bedroom has carpet, which keeps me nice and quiet. I crouch on the ground, my fingers pressed into the thick, fluffy, cream carpet. I can still hear the rustling. It sounds like someone is shuffling through papers.

Then—

'Aha!' someone whispers. I gulp and balance myself on my hands and knees, ready to crawl forward. Until, I hear an awful noise. I freeze. Someone is cutting something!

I hear the unmistakable clip of some scissors, the slow tearing of some paper. What on earth is going on out there? I glance behind me at the clock that sits above my bed. It's 5am!

'Agent Murphy,' I whisper to myself as I turn my attention back to the door. 'You have to be brave.'

I start to crawl forward but as soon as I do, the cutting

noise stops. The rustling resumes and I see something start to come under the door—some fingers pushing something through the small crack! I clap my hands to my mouth to stop me from yelling out. Then, as quick as they appeared, the fingers are gone. I hear the slight slap of someone's feet against the floorboards outside my door. They fade away, headed left down the hallway. Then a door creaks open and shuts silently.

A mobile phone light? That could be Grandma, Dad or Jimmy. Bare feet in the middle of winter? That rules out Grandma. Plus, the fact the person is up this early definitely makes me think Dad or Jimmy. But moving towards the left of the hallway and not the right where Dad's bedroom is? Why, Agent Murphy, I think we have our number one suspect, and his name starts with a J.

I stand up and walk towards the door. On the ground lies a cut out from a newspaper. I pick it up. The headline screams at me.

'ORIGIN OF A NEW ERA'.

There's a woman under the headline, dressed in a Queensland Maroons jersey, holding a football. She looks serious. She looks determined. Her name is Karina Brown. I notice the paper is fluttering in my hand. I realise it's because my hand is shaking.

I try to read the article but I'm too excited. I let the

important words sink in though: Women's State of Origin … Queensland … New South Wales … *tonight*. It sounds like my heart is beating inside my ears.

'Stand down, Agent Murphy,' I whisper. 'It appears our mystery is solved.'

Jimmy must have seen the newspaper on his way out for his usual morning run. I had no idea this was happening tonight. I sit down on my bed, unable to tear my eyes away from the article. It's still so early but I cannot sleep now. I have to watch this tonight.

But first I must get through a whole day of waiting. I have never wanted to go to school less in my life. Ugh.

***

Fifteen long hours later and I have finally made it. I swear everything Mrs Crawley said and did at school today was in slow motion. I spent most of my day staring at the clock.

But now, here I am. I'm planted on our fluffy rug, glued to the TV, my nose nearly touching the screen I am that close. It's State of Origin time … with a twist.

'And Studdon gets us underway for the second half. It's collected by Temara who gets it out to Hancock and WOW! That run shows us everything Origin is about, doesn't it?' the Channel Nine commentator bellows enthusiastically as the Queensland prop smashes into some NSW players.

I want to remember every word he says, every moment that happens in this game.

It is the women's State of Origin match and it is the most amazing thing I have ever seen. It's 6-all to start the second half. I've nearly chewed all my nails up in a mixture of excitement and nerves. I am wearing an old, battered Maroons jumper but as I watch the game, I want a new jersey. I want a women's one.

I want to be as classy as Queensland halfback Ali Brigginshaw. I want to be as fast as NSW fullback Samantha Bremner. I want to be as tough as Tazmin Gray and Simaima Taufa. I want to kick like Zahara Temara, take charge like Maddie Studdon, run like Annette Brander and tackle like Kezie Apps.

I'm pretty sure Jimmy himself has fallen in love with Queensland dummy-half Brittany Breayley. He's sitting on the couch behind me, yelling just as loudly, cheering just as proudly for the Maroons. When Brittany set up the first Queensland try for Karina Brown, he was more excited than I was. He always likes to watch the No.9 in any team and tonight, it's the same with the women.

'What do you think?' Jimmy asks me, as NSW get dangerously close to the try line.

'Ummm ...' is all I can manage as I watch the TV closely, too distracted to answer him.

100

He laughs but the laugh quickly turns to a groan as NSW cross for their second try and take the lead 10-6. I bury my head in my hands.

'C'mon Queensland,' I mutter to myself.

The next nine minutes are nerve-wrecking. Both teams come close so many times and I'm just not sure if Queensland are going to fight their way back.

Until—

'Brigginshaw, the star player, she steps through, Brown is with her, and Brown goes over for her second!' the commentator yells and this time I am yelling with him.

'YESSSSSS!' I scream as the Queensland girls celebrate. I'm jumping around with them. It's 10-all and we are back in the game.

'Sit down,' Jimmy laughs, throwing a couch cushion at me. 'I can't see!'

'Daniella,' a voice cuts through the room. I spin around. Dad is leaning up against the door frame to the lounge room, arms crossed. He doesn't look mad. He's not smiling but, in a weird way, it's like his eyes are doing the smiling for him.

'Listen to your brother and sit down, please. On the couch. You know you shouldn't sit so close to the TV.'

Geez. Ever since my concussion, Dad has become so

bossy. But I don't argue. I pick up the couch cushion, nod and run over to sit next to Jimmy. Dad remains in the doorway behind us, watching the game. I sneak a peek at Jimmy who glances at me sideways and does a teeny shrug. I smile and hug the cushion. Nothing can ruin this night for me. I feel brave.

'Do you see, Dad?' I ask, my heart slamming into my chest. 'Women can play too.'

I look over my shoulder at him. He sighs, looks at me, gives one little nod and walks away. At least I didn't get in trouble.

'Don't worry about it, kiddo,' Jimmy says. 'I have a feeling your day will come.'

I smile up at him and he puts his arm around me. But only for a second.

'Isabelle Kelly, we've all seen what she can do and here she comes again! She's going to present a challenge and OH! SHE'S OVER! Isabelle Kelly crashes over for her second try and I think NSW may have done just enough to secure this historic win,' the commentator screams. He seems delighted. But Jimmy and I are not. We both throw our arms up in the air.

'Noooo,' I yell. Tears actually sting my eyes. I so badly wanted Queensland to win. But the game goes to NSW, 16-10.

I lean forward, my elbows on my knees so Jimmy can't see how sad I am over a game of football.

'Jimmy,' I whisper as the final hooter sounds.

'Yeah, kiddo?'

'You reckon my day will come?'

'I do,' he says.

'Then help me,' I say, turning back to him. 'Help me show Dad and Grandma and everyone else that I can do that.' I point to the screen. 'I can be the next Sammy Bremner or the next Chelsea Baker. The next best fullback.'

'Not the next Kalyn Ponga?' he asks with a smile.

'Nup,' I say. 'I want to be just like them.'

As I look back at the screen, NSW captain Maddie Studdon lifts the shield high above her head with the biggest grin I have ever seen on anyone's face ever.

'I always say 'walk tall, stand proud, Murphy',' he says, as he puts his hand out to me for a fist bump. 'I'll see what I can do for you, kiddo. I'll see what I can do.'

CHAPTER THIRTEEN

MISSION: BECOME A RUGBY LEAGUE SUPERSTAR

The hum of the motorbike disappears down the street and I start the countdown in my head ... whose turn will it be today?

'One ... two ... three ... '

'Daniella!' Grandma calls out. I throw my head back, nearly dropping my book onto the doona. Ariana Grande plays through the speakers of my tablet. 'Get the mail please!'

I'm annoyed. Me?! I swear I've already done it a thousand times these school holidays and now they're taking me out of one of my happy places—reading a book while listening to music.

'Can't Jimmy do it?' I call back. I was at a really good point in my latest book—a mystery and a fantasy novel! Two of the main characters have just made a major discovery! All thanks to their female friend, of course. My only issue with this book so far is that the girl probably should have been the main character. I mean, it seems like it's always a pair of boys stumbling in the dark and only the girl thinks to bring a torch. But, of course, she is the one who is totally underestimated.

Jimmy appears in my doorway, tossing a footy between his hands.

'I did it yesterday, kiddo,' he teases. 'It's your turn.'

I sigh dramatically, chuck my book on my bed and stomp past him, hitting pause on Ariana's latest song. Getting the mail is one of the worst jobs because our driveway is so long. I'm also not in a great mood today because it's day seven of the winter school holidays and the twins are going crazy. They woke me up by throwing ping pong balls at my bedroom window and then hiding. When I finally got up, Sammy tried to wrestle me before I'd even eaten breakfast and then Tommy hid my book in the very back of Grandma's wardrobe, behind an old, stinky fur coat.

It took me an hour to find it because their only clues

were telling me if I was 'hot or cold' as I walked around the house. Every time I went near Grandma's room they lied and said I was 'cold'. It wasn't until Grandma made them tell me where it was that I found it.

They finally left me alone when they were allowed on the PlayStation to play Minecraft, but as I walk out the front door something big, furry and black falls onto me.

'EUGHHH,' I shout in alarm, doing a little dance to shake it off. A massive black spider falls to my feet.

'Spider!' I yell as I start stomping on it. Then I hear the bone-chilling laughter of my little brothers. They pop up from behind one of Dad's hedges.

'Got you,' Sammy teases.

'It's not even real, you loser,' Tommy laughs.

'You. Two. Are. Dead,' I say through clenched teeth.

'Thomas and Samuel, get here now,' Grandma calls down the hallway. She must have heard the ruckus. They both race past me, but not before Tommy flicks me behind the ear. I pick up the rubber spider and fling it down the hallway before slamming the door shut behind them.

I take a big breath and start to walk down the driveway, feeling the warmth of the bricks under my feet. I am still fuming about my brothers when out of nowhere, I get a funny feeling. It feels like someone is watching me. I spin back to look at the house and I swear I see a curtain twitch.

'What?' I whisper. A shiver runs up my spine. I keep staring at the house, but nothing else happens. Maybe it's Sammy or Tommy? But they'd be with Grandma by now. No, it must be my imagination. Maybe I need to take a break from all these mystery novels and do something else. It's making me see things that aren't there.

I continue down the driveway until I reach our brick letterbox. I open up the little door at the back and pull out three letters. There's a bill in a white envelope for Dad, a pink envelope for Grandma and a big yellow envelope for Agent Murphy. No. A manila envelope.

The white and pink envelopes are on the ground in seconds. I stare at the big one.

'TOP SECRET' is written across it in thick, red marker. 'AGENT MURPHY' is underneath, written slightly smaller in black. A 'top secret' assignment, perhaps?

Everyone but Grandma has the last name Murphy. It could be for anyone in our house. But I know it's for me. I'm Agent Murphy.

I flip it over and rip open the seal. Inside is a single sheet of white paper.

'I shouldn't read this out in the open,' I whisper to myself. No super-secret spy would make that mistake. I might have already compromised the mission. I look around. No one is near but it doesn't feel safe. I must follow agent protocol—get to a secure location.

I tuck the envelope under my shirt, scoop up the other two letters, and run up the driveway. I duck behind a tree every now and then, just in case someone is watching. I don't think I imagined the curtain moving before. Someone is onto me.

I don't go back into the house, but through the side gate that leads to the backyard. I press myself up against the cool brick of our home and peer around the corner.

The backyard is empty. Two bicycles lie unused on the grass—one is mine, the other is Tommy's from when we were riding yesterday. A load of washing hangs on the clothesline, swaying gently in the breeze. I can hear Sammy playing inside the house—'pew, pew, pew, pew' he calls out. The coast is clear, but where can I go?

I scan the yard again. Aha! The treehouse! I do one last sweep of the yard and then dash over to our big tree. I climb the wooden ladder nailed into the tree and slink into the wooden house. Chalk is on the ground from when the twins and I drew murals on the walls a few days ago. A stack of old rugby league magazines sit in one corner and three cushions are in the other. I walk over to the cushions and plonk myself down. I sneak one last peek through the ratty black curtains but see no one.

'All clear, Agent,' I whisper, slightly out of breath.

I settle in and finally take the white piece of paper out of the manila envelope.

AGENT NAME: Daniella Murphy

CODENAME: K1DD0

MISSION: BECOME RUGBY LEAGUE SUPERSTAR

WHEN: TUESDAY JULY 11

WHERE: BANFORD SAINTS RUGBY LEAGUE GROUNDS

YOUR MISSION: TO TRAIN WITH THE BANFORD SAINTS' UNDER-11s TEAM WHILE DAD AND GRANDMA WATCH. SHOW YOUR TALENT AND PROVE TO THEM THAT YOU CAN PLAY. COACH DONALD (CODENAME: SUPERCOACH) WILL BE YOUR LEADER ON THIS MISSION AND WILL BE EXPECTING YOUR ATTENDANCE.

SHOULD YOU CHOOSE TO ACCEPT, PLEASE REPORT TO AGENT JAMES (CODENAME: J1MMY) IN HIS BEDROOM AS SOON AS YOU FINISH READING THIS.

'He's actually done it,' I whisper to myself. It's been exactly two weeks since the women's State of Origin, two weeks since I asked for Jimmy's help once again. The paper flutters in my hand as I buzz with excitement.

Without even realising what I am doing, I am racing down the treehouse ladder, almost missing several steps in my rush. I tear towards the house, nearly tripping over my own bike, and rip open the back screen door.

'Walk inside, Daniella!' Grandma calls out from the computer room, where she is playing a game with Tommy. I slow down and pass Sammy's room, where he is still 'pew, pew, pewing' a fake gun at some stuffed alien toys. Finally, I reach Jimmy's room.

I knock three times.

'Come in,' he says.

I walk in and he is sitting on his bed, I think pretending to read a science textbook that he needs for next semester.

'Hello kiddo,' he says, a cheeky glint in his eye. 'Shut the door and then come and sit.' He gestures towards his desk chair. He's the only one who is allowed a computer in his own room since he's in high school and needs it for study.

I sit down and stare at him with wide eyes, desperate to hear his plan.

'I take it you received your mission?' he asks. I nod enthusiastically.

'Good,' he says. 'Here is how it's going to work. I spoke to Supercoach. He is happy for you to train with them for the rest of the year, if Dad and Grandma are OK with it. But it's too late to play this year as registrations are done. I don't think it's a bad thing though. It gives you the rest of the year to learn and then you can join next season all ready to go.'

My heart sinks a little but I nod. Jimmy is right. I have to make the best of the situation.

'Now, the under-11s train for an hour before my team, the under-16s. On this Tuesday, I am going to tell Dad and Grandma I am receiving a special award before training, at the same time the under-11s begin. That means Dad will have to come straight from work to make it in time and Grandma will have to pick you and the boys up after school and bring you to the grounds. I will take a bag of training clothes for you. You're to go straight to the sheds and get changed. Just tell Grandma you're going to play with other kids. Get your butt straight on the field before they can stop you. Show them what you can do. I will cop the heat when they realise what's happening. Deal?'

I swallow and it feels like there's a massive lump in my throat.

'Okay,' I say, sounding croaky.

'Now, I promised them I wouldn't help you train,' he continues. 'I am going to be in enough trouble for this plan as it is so I'm not going to break that promise. But you have just over a week so do what you can to prepare, okay? Come on morning runs with me and Dad, practise tackling a pillow or a big stuffed toy in your room, that kind of thing.'

I nod again.

'Thanks so much, Jimmy,' I say.

'No worries, kiddo. Just go out there and make me proud. Make the groundings we are going to get totally worth it.'

I laugh and nod.

'I will. My day has come,' I say.

CHAPTER FOURTEEN

YOU CAN'T BE WHAT YOU CAN'T SEE

My stomach is churning. My head is spinning. If I was a cartoon character, my face would be a very dark shade of green right now. Or maybe as white as a ghost.

I look around the grounds and everything seems so different. The ginormous gum tree looks evil and witchlike. The sky is grey and cloudy. The last time it looked like that, I ended up in hospital. No one is playing tiggy or chatting near the canteen. They're all huddled inside the clubhouse to escape the cold.

I've only just realised my own face is stinging in the wind. I guess I was too distracted by my urge to vomit to notice my face going numb. I'm not trying to be dramatic either.

It's THE day. Training day. My last chance to show Grandma and Dad that I belong on a rugby league field. So far, the plan has gone off without any hiccups. Dad and Grandma believed Jimmy's story about his special rugby league award and were very proud (which will be super awkward when there is no award).

Dad is on his way from work, Grandma picked Tommy, Sammy and me up from school and I have arrived at the Banford Saints rugby league grounds with 15 minutes to go until training starts. Jimmy found me when I arrived and is now walking me to the sheds where my bag is waiting for me—a Queensland Maroons backpack to keep me inspired. But as we make our way there, I am dizzy, my tummy is gurgling and my legs are as wobbly as jelly.

I look up and see Tyrone and Mitch and Bobby all tossing a ball around with the rest of the under-11s, waiting for training to start. I can't even begin to imagine their faces when I run onto the field with them. I walk past Coach Donald.

'Hurry up, Dani,' the coach says, pointing at his watch. It doesn't help. I can't even say anything back because I'm afraid I'll bring up my breakfast, morning tea and lunch all over his shoes.

I reach the doorway to the sheds, close my eyes and take a massive breath in. When I open them, there is one other person in there.

It's her.

'Surprise,' she says with a smile. Her red hair is tied back into a braid again. She's wearing a Gold Coast Titans t-shirt, Banford Saints shorts and black thongs. Her green boots, training socks and her black headgear sit on the bench next to her. It's Stephanie Annette Harden.

'Walk tall, stand proud, Murphy,' Jimmy whispers into my ear as he pushes me gently forward towards Stephanie.

'H-hey,' I say to her, with a small, awkward wave.

'Come on in,' she says. 'I have your bag. I can show you the best place to get dressed. My name is Steph.' She sticks her hand out. I fumble forward and shake it. No one ever shakes my hand, not unless we're making super-secret plans. It makes me feel like an adult.

'I'm Dani,' I reply. I no longer feel sick. My legs aren't shaking anymore and the dizziness is all gone. My food is safe in my stomach for now.

'Nice to meet you, Dani. Jimmy has told me all about you so I've been super excited to meet you. There are no other girls at this club so I think this is awesome! I really hope you play next year.'

I break out into a big smile.

'Really?'

'Yeah,' she says. She hands me my Maroons backpack and we walk to the back of the sheds where there are some toilet cubicles. She points into one and I go in, close the door and start getting changed.

'I started here this year after moving here from the Gold Coast. I played with a few girls down there but there's been none here so it's pretty cool you want to play too. Did you see the women's Origin?'

I nod before realising she can't see me.

'Yeah, I did,' I say, although it's a little muffled as I pull my training shirt on.

'That's my dream,' she says. 'One day I am going to play for the Queensland Maroons and the Australian Jillaroos and the Indigenous All Stars. Especially the All Stars.'

'Do the All Stars have women's teams too?' I ask, amazed.

'Yep,' she says. 'I want to be the Indigenous captain one day.'

'Well, I bet you will be,' I say as I pull my socks on. 'I've seen you play Steph and you're really good. You're so strong.'

I open the door and she tilts her head and smiles at me.

'Thanks a heap, Dani,' she says. 'Man, you look so good. I know you're going to smash it.'

I smile back. All my nerves are gone. Even if this is the last time I ever get to touch a football, I am going to make it all worth it. I walk forward and look at Steph.

'I know this is going to sound weird since we've only just met, but I want to thank you for inspiring me to play,' I say. 'You're a bit of a superhero to me.'

She looks momentarily shocked and then laughs.

'Wow. Well, thanks. I don't really know what to say … I don't think I've ever been anyone's superhero before,' she replies with a smile. 'But, you know, when my mum showed me the Indigenous All Stars women's game two years ago, she said to me that you can't be what you can't see. I watched that match and I saw what I could be. So, I think I understand exactly what you're saying. Now. Let's go!'

I follow Steph out of the sheds, my headgear in my hands. I give her a single wave goodbye as she walks over to the sidelines. I look around. I see Jimmy talking to Grandma, hopefully keeping her distracted. I see Tommy and Sammy running around with a couple of other kids near the ginormous gum tree. I look over to the carpark. Dad's blue ute isn't there yet. I'm half happy he's not here yet because I'm afraid he'll try to stop me before I get onto the field. But I'm also worried because he needs to be here to make this plan work.

Coach Donald comes up behind me.

'Are you ready, Dani?'

'I'm all good, coach,' I nod.

'Just call me Donald,' he smiles. We walk over to where the rest of the under-11s team is gathered and I see the surprise on the faces of my classmates. The members of the team that I don't know just look confused, maybe even a little suspicious. Tyrone however smiles at me and even Mitch manages a little grin but quickly hides it.

'Everyone, this is Dani Murphy,' Coach Donald says to the group. 'She's going to trial with us today and if she likes it, she's going to train with us for the rest of the year and hopefully play with us next year. Dani, this is the rest of the team. You'll get to know them as we go. Now everyone, out on the field for warm-ups.'

'Nice work, Dani!' Tyrone says as we walk towards the field. I glance back. I can see Grandma watching me with a confused frown on her face. Jimmy is looking over towards the car park. Still no Dad. Uh-oh.

***

'Okay, drinks break!' Coach Donald yells out.

I sigh, dropping the tackling pad. I suck in some big breaths. I'm bruised, I'm exhausted and yet, I feel wonderful. We're about halfway through the session and it's all been drills so far. Aside from a few tips on my tackling technique, I think I've been going really well.

I'm also on the opposite side of the field to Grandma and Jimmy, so I didn't have to hear the argument that I am sure they had when Grandma realised what I was doing. She's pacing up and down the sideline now, staring in my direction, while Jimmy is standing against the interchange bench, constantly looking over his shoulder to see if Dad is coming.

He's late. Either he knew what we were planning and is waiting at home for us to finish or he got stuck at work.

'Ok, let's split into two teams and run through some practice games,' Coach Donald says as everyone sips their water bottles dry. 'Dani, what kind of position do you think you'd like to play in the future?'

I sneak a guilty look at the team's fullback, Max Thompson.

'One day I'd like to be a fullback,' I say. Max laughs in a nice way and shrugs.

'I like some competition,' he says, grinning at me. I smile back.

'Hmmm, okay,' Coach Donald says, thinking about something. 'It's a tricky position to start with so today I'm going to put you on the wing, is that okay? It's a good step up to fullback.'

'Of course!' I say.

We all split into two teams and move into position. Sione is the centre on my team today, so at least he can't knock me out again.

As Max places the ball on the tee, ready to kick off, I hear a faraway yell. I turn back to the sideline and see Dad and Jimmy standing in front of the interchange bench with Grandma next to them. I can see Dad's frown from here. I feel like he's about to come carry me kicking and screaming off the field, but then I hear Jimmy yell back.

'Just watch her! Please, Dad. One practice game. Just watch her!'

I see Dad turn and look at me. As soon as he realises I am watching, his whole body relaxes but his eyes look sad. He looks back at Jimmy and then sits on the interchange bench. He stares back at me and holds up one finger.

One practice game. One last chance.

Coach Donald blows the whistle, Max kicks off and we run forward, ready to defend. Being on the wing, I don't see much action right away until a kid called Gareth sprints forward. Sione and I bring him down together. We go back and forth, set after set and I make a few more tackles and a few tiny runs, but nothing that shows I could be a rugby league superstar.

'Okay, last set and then we have a drinks break,' Coach Donald calls out. I know I haven't done enough to prove anything. I haven't looked at my family once this whole time. I'm afraid of how mad Dad will be, of how sad Grandma will be and how disappointed Jimmy will be that I have ruined this shot.

I look over at the other team. How can I beat them? I look at Tyrone, who is on my team and is about to play the ball to start the set. He sees me watching him and I just point at my chest.

Give me a chance, I think to myself, hoping the message somehow makes its way into his brain. He narrows his eyes and nods. Did he understand?

He plays the ball and Mitch swings it out to a big forward. Tackle one.

Mitch goes into dummy-half again and finds another big kid. Tackle two.

We've made some good metres but my time is running out. Then Tyrone calls out 'tackle three, to me!'.

Mitch passes the ball out to Tyrone, who quickly shoots it out to Sione and CRUNCH! The opposite centre tackles him into the ground. The ball didn't get to me. Tyrone tried, but it didn't make it.

'Tackle three,' Coach Donald calls out.

'Walk tall, stand proud, Murphy,' I whisper. I have to

take this chance for myself. No one else can save me now.

I run into dummy-half before Mitch can get there and I scoop the ball up from behind Sione. I dart forward, catching the opposition centre off guard as he tries to make his way back onside. I step past him, palm off the winger that's coming towards me and then, I'm in open space. I have a 40-metre run ahead of me. I pull my shoulders back and run tall.

'Go,' I whisper to myself.

Then I'm flying down the field. It's the fastest I have ever run. I can't feel my legs but I know they are moving, pushing me forward. I have the football tucked under my left arm and my wild ponytail is flapping around behind my head. I can feel someone chasing me, but they can't keep up. They're gone. I'm free. I've done it. I race under the posts to score my first ever try. The wind is squealing in my ears as I run, but over that I can hear a voice.

'Go, Dani! Go, Dani! Go!'

It's Dad.

CHAPTER FIFTEEN

MISSION ACCOMPLISHED

'The way you stepped past that centre was magic!' Jimmy howls as I walk towards him, taking my headgear off.

Training is over for me, and just starting for him, but we've come together on the halfway line. I'm scared to come off the field to face Dad and Grandma. I don't know if I'm ready to hear what they have to say. If I had a tent on me, I'd probably set it up and just live out here.

As we reach each other, Jimmy grabs me in his arms, picks me up and swirls me around.

'Put me down!' I shriek, but I'm laughing all the same.

'Kiddo, I have never been prouder. You did it. No matter what they say now, you showed your true potential,' he says, beaming at me.

'Thanks for this, Jimmy. Thank you for everything. You're the best big brother anyone could have.'

He ruffles my hair and winks.

'Good luck,' he says. 'Walk—'

'Walk tall, stand proud. I know, Jimmy,' I interrupt him. He just beams back at me, nods and runs off to join his team.

I take a deep breath in and look towards the sideline. Dad and Grandma are talking. They keep glancing in my direction. Dad looks a lot less mad than when he arrived. Grandma still looks a bit worried though. I know I have to get off the field eventually, so I muster up the courage and walk over to them.

'Okay,' I say as I approach. 'I know you're going to be mad and I know I'm probably going to be grounded until Christmas but I just wanted to prove to you guys what I could do.'

'Daniella,' Dad tries to cut in.

'No, wait. Please,' I say. It's almost like I can feel my heart beating throughout my entire body. 'Even if I never get to play again, I just want to know I did everything I could to at least try. I'm sorry if I've upset you guys but … but I'm not sorry that I did what I did.' I try to swallow but my throat is too dry. My palms are sweating and my body is shaking. Will they understand? 'Scoring that try was the best feeling in the whole world. Being part of that team was amazing. I had the best afternoon ever. I want to train with the under-11s for the rest of the year and then play with them next season in the under-12s if you let me.'

Dad and Grandma look at each other. I hold my breath.

'Let's go for a walk,' Dad says.

I grip my headgear, let my breath out and give them a little nod. I start to bite my fingernails as the three of us head towards the car park. We come out on the street and walk along the footpath, away from the fields. What little sun could be seen from behind the clouds is starting to completely disappear now and all the trees that line the pathway make it seem even darker.

'The only reason your Grandma and I didn't want you to play was because we wanted to keep you safe, Dani,' Dad starts. I look up at him, but he's staring ahead as he walks. I look at Grandma who is watching me and gives me a little smile. I see some tear marks in her makeup. Oops. I must have scared her.

'We want you to understand that first and foremost. We weren't trying to be strict or mean, although we understand it's probably come across that way. We just wanted you to be safe.'

'I understand,' I say.

'Secondly, while we understand you felt you had to keep it a secret at the start, we didn't appreciate the lies. We are not happy about the lies today, either. You and your brother will both be grounded for another month each for this stunt you pulled today.'

Uh-oh. He sounds mad again. I can handle the grounding. But is he about to ban me from football for life AGAIN?

'But finally,' he says, as he stops walking and turns to face me, 'finally, your Grandma and I have come to an agreement. You can continue to train with the under-11s for the rest of the year. You must continue to learn from Jimmy, especially your tackling techniques. And then, next year, you can sign up to play. But, you have to promise you're going to practise, you're going to learn and you will always wear headgear, even if it's just in the park.'

I am stunned. My whole body feels numb. I look at Grandma, who is still smiling at me. I look at Dad and spot tears in his eyes.

'You were very good today, Dani,' he says. 'You were a natural. I'm just scared of you getting hurt. But I'm also scared of Jimmy and Tommy and Sammy getting hurt and I don't stop them from playing so I shouldn't stop you either. We shouldn't treat you any differently just because you're a girl and we're sorry it took us a while to understand that. We also think your Mum would be pretty mad at us right now. She always lived her life to the fullest and she would have wanted you to do the same.'

He wipes away one little tear that has escaped from his eye.

'I won't let you down, Dad,' I whisper. 'Or Mum or Grandma. Thank you so much.'

Then I burst into happy and relieved tears. I run forward and pull them both into a hug. I can hear Grandma laughing, a beautiful tinkly laugh.

'Oh Daniella,' she says. 'How you remind me of your mother.'

She bends down and puts her hands on my cheeks.

'You're so determined. You're so stubborn. But you're so talented. And I'm sorry that I stopped you from chasing your dreams. I should have listened to you more but I won't get in your way anymore. You go for those dreams, my girl.'

I smile back at her as I remember our conversation about our dreams. I hug her and breathe in her lavender scent.

'I'm still your little girl,' I say.

'I know,' she says back.

'Alright,' Dad says. 'That's enough tears for now. Let's

get back to the clubhouse before Tommy and Sammy burn it down.'

I laugh then take both their hands and walk between them back to the rugby league grounds. I feel like I'm floating. Is this even real?

I look up at Dad.

'Dad, I love you,' I say.

He laughs.

'I love you too, Dani.'

***

To: soccer.star@mailbox.com

From: dani.number1@mailbox.com

Subject: WATCH OUT WORLD!

AMINA AMINA BO-BINA! GUESS WHAT?! MY DAD AND MY GRANDMA HAVE FINALLY AGREED TO LET ME PLAY RUGBY LEAGUE!! That's right. You're now talking to the next rugby league superstar … even if it is just the superstar of the Banford Saints under-12s team hahaha. I get to play with them from next year. I finally showed everyone what I can do. I AM SO EXCITED!!

To: dani.number1@mailbox.com

From: soccer.star@mailbox.com

Subject: Re: WATCH OUT WORLD!

DANI DANI BO-BANI! THAT IS THE BEST

NEWS EVER!! I'M SO PROUD OF YOU DANI! I need you to tell me the whole story. I wish I could come to Queensland to watch you play but one day you'll be a rugby league superstar and I'll be a soccer superstar and together, we will rule the WORLD! Kick some butt Dani!

CHAPTER SIXTEEN

EIGHT MONTHS LATER

I see the ginormous gum tree, its leaves swaying gently in the wind. A bunch of kids sit nearby, playing duck, duck, goose. Some parents stand in a line near the canteen, waiting to get their hands on hot chips and burgers before the game starts. A rather skinny man with no hair barks orders at his players as they run through their warm-up on the side of the field. The players run in a line, bringing their knees to their chest. One boy counts as they go.

There is football noise all around me and it is the greatest feeling ever. Because, tonight, I am making my debut for the Banford Saints under-12s team. It's our first game of the season.

It's autumn. The sun is almost completely gone, the big lights above the field shine brightly, the smell of the greasy canteen food wafts through the air.

I'm standing in the doorway of the dressing sheds and I can see all my favourite people. I see Grandma sitting in her fold out chair on the sideline. She is wearing a purple shirt with the number 1 stitched into it in red. Number 1. My number. She made it herself. Jimmy stands next to her, pacing every now and then, fidgeting with his hands, pushing his thick hair around his head. I can tell he's excited and nervous for me. We've done a lot of work to get here. His first game of the year is on Sunday. Tonight it's all about me. Even Tommy and Sammy are on the sideline, swinging their bodies around the railings that border the field. But they're here, ready to watch me play.

Steph and Bethany sit a little further up, on a long bench. Steph has had to join a new club because she's under-13s now and needed an all-girls team. She found one and is happy but promised to cross back onto enemy territory tonight to see my debut. Bethany didn't even need an invite to come. She declared last year that she would be at every game and even made herself some crepe paper pom-poms. She is filming tonight's game with her family's spare mobile phone so that Amina can watch it later.

And then there's Dad. He is wearing the red and blue colours of the Banford Saints, filling up water bottles at the outside tap. He's my team's trainer. He has been a trainer for Jimmy, Tommy and Sammy before. This year, he's with the under-12s. He's with me.

I think back to this time last year when I made my NRL season predictions and snuck in my random prediction of me playing rugby league. The Broncos didn't win the premiership, Queensland didn't win Origin and Kalyn Ponga wasn't the Dally M Player of the Year. My random prediction was the only one I got right. I didn't win the $20. But I won something much better. My chance to play football.

'Okay team, let's go!' Coach Donald barks. I step back from the doorway of the sheds as captain Tyrone heads to the front of the line to lead the team out.

It's time to move.

'You've got this Murphy,' Tyrone winks.

'Thanks Ty!'

I walk down to find a place in the line. Mitch Delaney turns around and gives me the thumbs up. I shoot him one back.

'Let's go Saints!' Tyrone yells from the front.

'Up the Saints!' we all yell back.

I pull my headgear on, tightening the strap under my chin. My boots crunch on the concrete ground underneath me as we walk through the door. As soon as I hit the grass,

I jog forward onto the field. The big lights sparkle above. The cold air hits me. The cheers echo around me.

This is it. I've made it.

ACKNOWLEDGEMENTS

To the team at Wombat — particularly Rochelle, Sara and Anita — thank you for taking a chance on me and this book, and for helping me craft it into what I had always hoped it could be.

To Craig Cauchi, the team at Queensland Writers Centre, and my excellent Publishable mentor Lee McGowan, thank you for seeing the worth in my work and steering me in the right direction when I needed it the most.

Thank you to those (past and present) at The Courier-Mail, Sunday Mail and QWeekend who have helped me achieve my dreams as a sports journalist. Special mentions to Kristy, Smokey, KP, Al, Laura, Alison, Emma, Vanessa, Stanno and Rosie – your belief, advice, opinions and friendships over the years mean more to me than I think you know.

To Julie Farrell, Donna Fedrick, Bob Huntley-Chipper and Chris White, thank you for reading, guiding me, and being among the first I could trust with this little dream of mine.

To Emily Hayes — all your support means the world and I only hope that one day I can return the favour to help you achieve your goals. Thank you, little bookworm.

To my extended families — Arnold, Hayes and Lahey — especially my grandparents, who have followed my career, my NRL tips, and even read my half-baked stories when I was seven years old. I will always treasure your support.

Big love and thank you to my Dad, Danica, Chloe and Zach. You are my rocks in life and with everything I do, I hope I make you all proud. Sam, thank you for the feedback, ideas and title. Sustaining my career since 2009.

To my Mum, thank you for answering countless questions, for reading, for brainstorming, and for your constant love and guidance. Thank you for just being there. There are no words to sum up my gratitude, but I know I can count on you. I love you.

And of course, to my husband Tim — your love, encouragement and gentle pushing has kept me going and I know I wouldn't have been able to do this without you. You're the best teammate I could ever have. To my boys, Patrick and Charlie, you're the reason I strive to do better every day and I love, love, love you both so very much.

And finally, to Tallisha Harden and Steph Hancock. Thank you for opening my eyes. You are where it all started for me and I'm forever in your debt.

To Rebecca Stanton, thank you for being the first one to ever show me just how powerful a girl can be on a footy field.

And to Ali, Meg, Karina, Tazmin, Zahara, Annette, Chelsea L, Chelsea B, Jamie-Lee, Simaima, Amber, Amelia, Julia, Heather, Renee, Karyn, Colleen, Mary K, Fiona, Katie, Alicia and the countless many, many more (I'm so sorry I can't name you all!) — thank you for being the trailblazers, the leaders and the legends that you are. Thank you for sharing your stories with me and working alongside me.

This book is for you all and for the future generations.

About the Author

Rikki-Lee Arnold has been writing books since the age of seven, when she would spend her Saturday mornings creating worlds and characters while watching *Rage* and *Video Hits*. These days she is also a sports journalist and has worked through her decade-long career at *The Courier-Mail* and *Sunday Mail* covering NRL, women's league, tennis, AFLW, cricket and more. Her combined love of writing and sports – particularly women's sport – has led to her debut novel, *The First Tackle*. Rikki-Lee lives in Brisbane with her supportive husband and her two cheeky sons.